# Please
# Omit
# Funeral

*By Hildegarde Dolson*

*Mysteries*
PLEASE OMIT FUNERAL
A DYING FALL
TO SPITE HER FACE

*Other Books*
HEAT LIGHTNING
OPEN THE DOOR
WE SHOOK THE FAMILY TREE
GUESS WHOSE HAIR I'M WEARING
THE GREAT OILDORADO
SORRY TO BE SO CHEERFUL
THE FORM DIVINE
HOW ABOUT A MAN?
THE HUSBAND WHO RAN AWAY
A GROWING WONDER

*With Elizabeth Stevenson Ives*
MY BROTHER ADLAI

# Please
# Omit
# Funeral

## HILDEGARDE DOLSON

J. B. LIPPINCOTT COMPANY
Philadelphia and New York

Lines are quoted from "Cuttings (Later)" and "Orchids,"
copyright 1948 by Theodore Roethke, from
*The Collected Poems of Theodore Roethke.*
Used by permission of Doubleday & Company, Inc.


U.S. Library of Congress Cataloging in Publication Data

Dolson, Hildegarde.
    Please omit funeral.

    I.  Title.
PZ3.D6964Pl   [PS3507.O662]   813'.5'4   74-30007
ISBN-0-397-01081-8

For Dick

# Please
# Omit
# Funeral

# 1

Wingate, Connecticut, which lies fifty concrete miles north of New York, has some of the loveliest old Colonial houses anywhere—and some of the busiest reactionaries. Historians mention Wingate in their books not because a few minor battles of the American Revolution were fought there, but because in one of them Benedict Arnold's horse was shot out from under him. This was before he became a traitor, but if Benedict Arnold had had any such intentions that early in the Revolution, he could have found plenty of sympathizers in Wingate. Many Tories even painted a black band around their chimneys so that the British would know who their friends were.

Modern-day Wingate residents of the fanatically Tory cast of mind no longer paint a black band around their chimneys, which is, in some ways, a pity, though it might be a scary sight for the badly outnumbered liberals. Deprived of a King George the Third to rally to, they do their loyal best to elect presidents who will act like kings and to stamp out dissent wherever it raises its hydra head. In the past four or five years they have become even more convinced of their mission to protect America from Americans who think the wrong way. Their clubs, societies, and *Bunds* have multiplied. And individual members who feel things are moving too slowly, because of tiresome obstacles such as the U.S. Constitution, can always make an end run around the Opposition.

On an early May afternoon, the founder and chairwoman of one of these right-thinking groups, Mrs. Georgina Hampter, parked her car on a back road above and a quarter mile behind the new high school and waited impatiently. Waiting was not her long suit, and waiting on an inconspicuous back road—a muddy road, at that—was so unnatural as to make her even more impatient.

The car was a black Lincoln Continental, which may have had some tenuous affinity with the Tory sympathizers' black-banded chimneys. The new high school, which was built of enormous glass slabs in rectangles connected by covered passageways, had no affinity whatever with Wingate's historical past or architecture. Lucy Ramsdale, another resident of Wingate several miles removed, had taken one look at the glassily squared-off façade and remarked, "It proves that ice cubes should never copulate."

Georgina Hampter approved of the school's sanitary glassiness, but she was implacably against some of the things going on inside. As she sat in her Lincoln Continental, fuming and tapping her large, expensively shod foot, she at least had the satisfaction of knowing she was doing something positive to correct what was wrong.

Her reluctant messenger (he was really too young and stupid to be called a spy) was at that moment jogging through a loggia toward the high school library. Ronnie Ellis was jogging partly because he was late in carrying out secret instructions and partly because jogging was more natural to him than putting one foot flatly in front of the other. Springy-balls-of-the-feet was his style. He had had a good sweaty workout with the track team on the athletic field given by Georgina Hampter's late husband, the razor blade tycoon. Then he had jogged to the locker room to shower and change into more suitable attire than track pants for his delicate assignment.

He was now wearing blue jeans and a white sweat shirt modestly emblazoned across the front, in royal blue, WINGATE WINS. He was a knobby-boned boy, and his chest did nothing to swell out the WINGATE WINS. This was just as well because his mother, a disciple of Georgina Hampter, had recently been given a magazine article by Georgina that said habitual users of marijuana were apt to get overdeveloped breasts more suitable to females, and Georgina had advised the mother to watch for this telltale stigma among her son's friends to make sure he wasn't falling into evil company. It had been rather embarrassing for Ronnie, whenever a pal came to the house, to have his mother stare fixedly at a point, or points, several inches below the newcomer's chin, as if she were some kind of nipple nut. Ronnie himself had smoked a few joints but had decided it cut down on his wind.

As he approached the library, he was in such an apprehensive state he would have welcomed the chance to have a few more private, soothing drags. He had never felt at home in the library, and on his infrequent visits he had certainly never lingered there. But now, as he came in, he looked enviously at the four or five students reading in the pleasant lounge near the entrance. They sat or sprawled on the two big green vinyl sofas or in the matching easy chairs, with newspaper and magazine racks comfortably at hand. A half-dozen other students sat at tables out in the main room, making notes from books piled in front of them. As Ronnie walked past, he scrunched into himself and ducked his already receding chin, as if that would make him invisible, but a girl from his biology class glanced up and said, "Hi, Ronnie," and he had to croak "Hi." The fluorescent lighting which covered the entire ceiling and gave the effect of clear daylight seemed as glaring to him as a spotlight.

He had hoped one of the student helpers would be on duty at the circulation desk, but it was empty. The classmate who'd said "Hi" pointed toward the far side of the room. "She's over there."

He looked and saw Miss Coving, the librarian, up on a ladder hanging photographs on the wall above the card catalog. They were a series of mounted glossies from a recent Joe Papp production of *Two Gentlemen of Verona* and they had no interest for Ronnie, whose idea of a picture worth studying was the centerfold nude in *Playboy* magazine. (He kept one of these hidden under the lining paper in his bottom bureau drawer and only got it out late at night to accompany him in Portnoyish procedures his mother would have considered the sure road to depravity and/or insanity.)

If the Shakespearean characters bore marked dissimilarities to a *Playboy* centerfold, so did the librarian, in that she wore clothes and had a more intelligent forehead. But in many ways, young Miss Coving, like the *Playboy* models, was a bird to fly with. Ronnie, who had been a junior lifeguard at the town beach the summer before, had seen her in a bikini and admired her figure sincerely, if silently. Neither he nor his friends ever whistled out loud at Miss Cov-

12

ing, however much they whistled inside. She was not only the librarian, which carried an aura of bookishness, but she was always at the beach with Mr. Solent, who taught Drama and Film Studies and, more to the point, fencing, being a very fast man with a sword.

Looking at Miss Coving's back view now, as she balanced on the ladder, Ronnie was sorry to involve her in what he had to do, although not nearly as sorry as he was about having to involve himself. He pushed his unwilling legs to the circulation desk, reached around a vase of forsythia, and tapped the bell, which gave out a soprano *ping*.

Miss Coving got down off the ladder—even stepping backward, she was quick and graceful—and came across the room. She was wearing an apple green pants suit, and her hair, which was the pale yellow of a newly sliced moon, was pulled back severely and tied in a hank. On her, it didn't look severe.

"Hello, Ronnie, will you be at the beach again this summer?" Her voice was soft and slightly husky.

The boy's nerves were so exacerbated he had almost expected her to snap, "What are you doing in here? You haven't used the library in months. Don't you try any tricks."

Her remembering him from the beach made him feel even worse. He gulped and produced the list from his back pocket. "I want to take out these books."

Students were trained, early and firmly, to look up titles in the card catalog and find their own books, but Marcy Coving had a mental picture of Ronnie wandering openmouthed, lost in a wilderness of dark bindings and Dewey Decimals. She couldn't bear to think of it. She had been hired, a newly hatched Master of Library Science, as an assistant and had been promoted precipitately when the head librarian re-

13

signed to follow an engineer husband being transferred. She had a loving sense of possession about *her* library and knew every statistic by heart: forty-one books per pupil, which meant over forty-nine thousand books, give or take a few dropouts; a magazine collection on microfilm going back eleven years; one thirty-five-millimeter and one sixteen-millimeter projector and one record player for each classroom, stored in *her* care, with records and film, to be locked up every night. She could have found any single item instantly, in the stacks or the storage room, and she reached for Ronnie's list with no feeling of being put upon. She was glad to help him discover a new world.

When she looked at the first title on his list, she was even gladder. "I think you'll love *Wayward the World*. I read it the first time when I was your age, and it's been one of my favorites ever since." She was twenty-four, so she could afford to sound ancient. "You know, the author, Lawrence Dilman, lives near Wingate."

The unknown (to Ronnie) Dilman might live near Wingate, but Georgina Hampter lived nearer.

"I tried to get Mr. Dilman to speak to our Literary Club last winter, but his wife said he'd been very sick."

Ronnie wasn't sorry to hear this. In fact, he would have preferred all the authors on the list to be safely dead, so as not to make trouble.

He shuffled his feet to indicate haste was desirable. He was so edgy he almost hopped up and down on one foot.

Marcy Coving, having looked over the other six titles on the paper, was thinking that it was a very mixed bag of books. "Did your teachers recommend these or is it your own list, Ronnie?"

14

In that he had copied off Georgina Hampter's titles in his own laborious handwriting, this was his list. He managed to croak, "Mine."

"Several of these have been withdrawn from use in classes because the school board considered them too controversial." Unconsciously, her pretty nose wriggled as if she'd smelled putrid fish. "They've been retained in the library, but we've been asked to make clear to students that if your parents have any objection to your taking these books, you may choose alternates for supplementary reading. You do understand that, don't you?"

Ronnie said, rather desperately, "My mother *wants* me to take them."

# 2

On a Friday afternoon in mid-May, Lucy Ramsdale and her weekend guest were sitting on the terrace in that slightly glutted state old friends get into when they haven't seen each other for years and have gobbled course after course of nostalgia. (Both had been young wives and career climbers in Greenwich Village before high-rise rabbit warrens took over.) Lucy, who usually had an ardent grip on the present, had kept the do-you-remember going longer than she normally would because (1) it was a comforting escape from a Now suddenly, treacherously, gone sour and (2) it kept her guest from asking awkward questions about the absence of Inspector McDougal, Lucy's tenant in the studio behind the house.

Alison Moffat was sitting a few feet away in the solidest, best-padded chair on the terrace. She had two chins now, and massive hips, and in spite of having lived in allegedly sunny California for most of the past twenty years, her face had the thick whiteness of dough, sprinkled here and there with liver spots like cinnamon. As she lay back dozing, making whiffling sounds, Lucy looked at her and felt that human mixture of resentment and compassion and superiority because an old friend has aged so unsuitably. Alison, with her magnificent eyes closed and her delicious speaking voice mute, the voice she'd used to play comedy lines to perfection—this Alison was so defenseless Lucy couldn't bear to look any longer. She reached for the *Wingate Bugle,* which had been delivered just as she was about to serve a lobster salad for lunch. For news on a global scale, she would no more have done without the *New York Times* than without coffee at breakfast. But for local matters, or almost any happenings in and around Fairfield County, the *Bugle,* a weekly, was irreplaceable.

On page 1, Lucy read with satisfaction that Nature had finally struck back at the spanworm by sending wasps whose sole, splendid purpose in life was to sting and render harmless the eggs from which the worms hatched. The summer before, worms had feasted on almost every tree on her eleven acres. As she thought of this, it conjured up too vividly in her artist's mind a picture of Inspector McDougal going forth, in a squashy old felt hat and high boots, to swat and sweep the writhing black curtain of worms hanging on the front and back doors and on the French doors opening onto the terrace. He'd filled a huge garbage can. It wasn't a romantic picture; nothing in her relationship with McDougal was romantic. Yet his being there had filled so solid a place in her life that to have him gone left her feeling as if somebody had sawed her in two and botched the job of putting her back together.

She skipped from the worms to a headline that gave her a Cassandra glow of I-told-you-so: NEW COMPUTERIZED TRAFFIC LIGHTS ON MAIN STREET STAY RED FOR 3 HOURS—MASSIVE TRAFFIC JAM. Lucy's opinion of computers had been conveyed, forcibly, to Chief of Police Salter, to Sergeant Terrizi, and, above all, to her tenant, Inspector McDougal, who had cravenly ducked the issue by saying he was only a homicide man. Now her blackest prophecies had come true, but the triumph of I-told-you-so was tarnished by not having anybody on hand to say it to—or to refrain from saying it to, which was sometimes even more fun.

She glanced driftily at the next column: LOCAL CITIZEN DESTROYS BOOKS FROM SCHOOL LIBRARY. . . .

Suddenly, she took in what she was seeing, and as she went on to the first paragraph, her adrenaline surged up like sap:

> Mrs. A. G. Hampter, who was defeated for re-election to the school board last November, enlisted the aid of a student in Wingate High earlier this month, to remove several controversial books from the school library. She then destroyed them. This came to light when the student's mother sent in a check to cover the cost of the books, which she claimed had been lost by her son. Miss Marcy Coving, the librarian, became suspicious, and her investigation soon determined—Continued on page 6.

Lucy, muttering ominously, turned to page 6: the first thing she saw was the headline of an advertisement that took up three columns, twenty inches deep.

SHALL WE POLLUTE OUR CHILDREN'S MINDS?

Her outraged yip brought Alison awake.

"That damn Hampter woman's riding her broomstick again. We got her defeated for the school board by making everybody who came into the Thrift Shop sign a petition backing Jenny Wright so we could get Jenny on the ballot."

Lucy modestly neglected to say that several of her fellow volunteers at the Thrift Shop, all ultra Republicans, had accused her of singlehandedly turning a charitable organization into a political arena. One had even accused Lucy of marking down price tags for petition signers, but since Lucy was much more popular than her accuser, this charge never really got far.

She was giving her guest a small background briefing. ". . . even most of the conservatives on the school board wouldn't vote to remove the books from the library, so now Georgina's had them sneaked out and thrown down her incinerator or something." She rattled the paper commandingly. "Listen to this bilge water: 'Shall we pollute our children's minds?' "

"How could we pollute children's minds these days?" Alison asked reasonably. "Like carrying coals to Newcastle."

A Broadway critic had once written, "When Alison Moffat throws a line away, it comes back like the loaves and fishes, a miraculous bounty of laughter."

At the moment, Alison's audience of one was too engaged to react suitably. She was skim-reading the rest of the advertisement, relaying the bits that made her maddest: " 'We pay taxes for sewers to carry away contaminating filth. . . . Must we also pay taxes for schools that assign contaminating filth as reading matter? . . . Citizens for a Clean-Minded Community say No! Our chairwoman, Mrs. Georgina Hampter, urges all taxpayers and parents who feel that filth must go— *and not be replaced*—to come to the meeting Monday night. Support her action and call or write the . . .' Mmmm." Lucy was reading to herself now.

"What books has she put on the bonfire?"

"Let's see. . . . *Grapes of Wrath.* . . ."

"They burned that in North Dakota last month. Steinbeck would be flattered to know what a hot item he is."

"Eldridge Cleaver's *Soul on Ice.* . . . Oh, my God!" Her voice had shot up half an octave. "Guess who's banned—Lawrence Dilman's *Wayward the World!* Poor Larry. That ought to give him a shot in the arm. He's been feeling so out of things. Remember when he was writing it in the place across from us on Perry Street, and he used to dangle their baby out the window on a rope?"

"In the market basket—or was it a dog basket?—to give the little thing fresh air." Alison made a cradling cup with both hands, the long, unexpectedly slim hands she'd used so effectively on stage and in films for over thirty years. "Willard and I used to have breakfast on our balcony right opposite that window, and whenever the basket swayed in the breeze, Willard had nervous vibrations."

"I should think it would have made Larry's wife even more nervous. What was her name, Ginny?"

"Let's see. Wife Number One. I get them confused unless I line them up in chronological order. Yes, Ginny. I remember because she never drank gin. But she didn't sit there and watch her child dangling four flights up. She was always off working in some dreary office, supporting Larry while he was writing *Wayward the World.* And to do him justice, he worked like a dog on that book. He didn't have time to wheel the baby down to Washington Square every morning."

"He could have worked at night. I told him so." Lucy, who had only one chin, and that prettily pointed, set it in stern, or relatively stern, lines. "Children should feel secure." As a childless widow, she could sound especially authoritative. "And how could that baby feel secure dangling on a rope? I told Larry off."

Alison looked at her old friend with amusement. "Hal used to say, 'Lucy likes to tell people what to do, but not for their own good—for hers.'"

At the mention of her husband, who had died several years before, Lucy's vivid little face softened. In her sixties, she still had the finely whittled bones of a beauty, and the charm of a woman who never has to try to be charming. "Hal used to defuse me regularly before I exploded in the wrong place." Her eyes sparkled with laughter. "But he couldn't stop me from blasting Larry. I marched right over there and said what I thought of him."

"How did our glamour boy react?"

"He laughed and said it was more interesting to kiss a pretty woman when she was fighting mad." Lucy snorted. "He tried—and I kicked him."

"I didn't kick him. Not till much later." Alison stared up at a spider swinging from a low branch of the ash tree over the terrace. "I came after Wife Number Two."

Lucy was startled speechless, a rare state for her. She had never thought of Alison as a woman who might attract men like Larry. Even in her peak acting days, Alison had been a big woman: big breasts, strong short neck, beaky nose that seemed exactly right for the rather majestic head. Offstage, she had always looked like one of those large packages no one can quite wrap up properly, so that bits stick out in odd places, and the whole thing needs patching with gummed tape. (Alison had often used safety pins.)

At parties, she was both feted and feared—feted because she was witty and a marvelous mimic, feared because her tongue could jab out as suddenly and sharply as a switchblade.

Lucy thought, Larry must have taken it as an amusing challenge. But with Alison, it would go much deeper. She said slowly, "You certainly hid it well. I never guessed."

"You and Hal moved up here just before it started. And Willard wouldn't have known either, but Larry deliberately left a letter of mine out on a table for Willard to see, then made a big thing about hiding it —'guilty lover covering up' act. To him, Willard was a thick-skinned, stolid businessman and he couldn't resist puncturing that."

There was something unbearably sad, to Lucy, about seeing Alison's liver-spotted hands, with the expressive fingers, clench and unclench. "We all loved you so much more than we did Willard. He never had a tenth of your quality."

"But he was *right* for me. That's what none of you realized. He wasn't thick-skinned; he was solid and kind and unassuming and totally honest. And he'd always encouraged me to hog the limelight in public. That's damn rare in a man. But after he found out about Larry and me, he turned to his secretary for comfort. And she comforted him all the way to the altar. That first winter after the divorce was hell. Larry went up to lecture at Sarah Lawrence, and one of his adoring students became Wife Number Three. The adoration of the young always went to his head. Or should I say to his groin?" The forced laugh was like a parody of the famous throaty gurgle that had enchanted audiences. "It's ludicrous to think that once

I wanted to kill him. I used to run into him later in Hollywood, but I haven't seen him in years." She shifted her bulky hips as if to ease a physical ache. "Well, that was long ago and far away, and now the wench is buried in whale blubber. Larry wouldn't know me if he saw me."

"Nonsense. And he leaped at the chance to see you again. We're going there for dinner tonight."

Alison heaved herself up in one wrathful surge. "Lucy! You had no right to involve me. You said it would be a quiet weekend. Call Larry and tell him I'm sick. I *am* sick. My blood pressure's hideous. And it's too hot out here. I should have stayed in my air-conditioned room at the Barclay." She gave another heaving motion that got her out of the deck chair; once on her feet, she moved quite briskly toward the French doors opening into the living room.

It wasn't too hot. At three o'clock of that mid-May afternoon, the breeze came greenly fresh from the woods behind Lucy's house, although in Wingate proper, three miles away, it was ten degrees warmer. Lucy had done her marketing there early, before she met Alison's train, and marketed rather sketchily, for so good a cook and hostess. She had felt newly blah about food, and thankful that she and her guest were invited out for dinner.

As she followed Alison into the house, into the big, light, uncluttered living room, her mind split and raced in two diverging channels: what to haul out of the freezer for dinner if they had to stay home; how to persuade her guest not to cancel the evening out.

Alison had settled herself on the olive-green love seat. She didn't actually take up the full width, but she was a woman who commanded the space around her.

Compared to her, Lucy Ramsdale looked as fragile as porcelain, a look that was often as useful as it was ornamental, especially around men. She perched on a needlepoint stool and smiled up at her friend. "You're right. It *is* better inside. And I didn't mean to railroad you into anything. I just thought it would be dull for you to have a whole weekend alone with me."

"It's exactly what I wanted."

But it's not what I wanted, Lucy thought resentfully. I'm in the dumps, and I need something more than another old woman. (It was a sign of how low she was feeling that she'd think of herself, even tangentially, as old.) She always enjoyed parties, but there were times when it was more than that, when she craved them as nourishment, to feed her ego, to release a fresh spurt of the affection and curiosity and gaiety she felt in company.

Alison, as if remembering this from years past, said she was sorry if she'd sounded like a party poop. "But I simply can't take parties any more. I can't stand excitement. With my blood pressure, I'd pop like a balloon."

"Not at Larry's. He had a coronary or something last year, and he goes on like the Ancient Mariner about it. He'll give you his entire medical history, probably illustrated with slides. You should see what he's currently married to."

"What? A fifteen-year-old hoyden?"

"A cardiovascular X-ray technician." Lucy's voice rang with triumph. "She's crisp and wholesome and arch-preserved. I keep expecting her to say, 'Draw a deep breath and hold it.'"

"You've invented her just to cheer me up."

"So help me." Lucy did a cross-my-heart with the sturdy, blunt-fingered artist's hand that was oddly at variance with the rest of her. "Barbara ran the cardiac machine or something when Larry was having his heart attack. Maybe he married her so she could take his cardiograms at home and he wouldn't have to keep running back to the hospital. She's one of those women with sensible ankles."

Alison stretched like an oversize cat and contemplated her lower extremities as if she were going to lick herself; for a bulky woman, her legs and ankles were surprisingly good.

"She's a health-foods fanatic—wheat-germ-'n'-yogurt sort. And she got Larry to give up smoking and drinking."

"Good God, the emperor is naked. He has nothing to do with his hands." Alison added hopefully, "Is he bald and flabby too?"

"N-no." Lucy would have liked to paint a bald, flabby ex-lover to make her old friend even happier, but she still had hopes of getting Alison to see him, so fibbing wasn't feasible at the moment. "But he has a dulled-down look." She got rather carried away. "Like a long, limp vegetable that's been left out in the sun." That would explain the tan.

"Well, after all, he's pushing Medicare. He's around our age."

"Speak for yourself. You're six years older than I am."

"And I look twenty years older."

Lucy protested loyally, but privately she agreed. And she couldn't help feeling a childish sense of grievance because her friend wasn't being more entertaining. It was as if Alison had brought the contagious germ of old age with her, just when Lucy, usually so impervious, was most vulnerable. She thought drearily, As if I weren't low enough this weekend.

"You're one of the main reasons I came east," her guest said. "I wanted to see you again before I die."

Lucy was so concerned she sounded cross. "Don't talk like that. You have years and years yet. Everybody lives longer now."

"That's the trouble. It's like pollution—the more we progress, with all our clever new inventions, the more we pollute. And now we've made so much progress medically we'll have more and more creaking old zombies around. If doctors insist on stretching out our life span synthetically, by unnatural means, then we're justified in ending it whenever we've had enough."

"I hate this kind of talk." Lucy's voice quivered. "You make me feel as if I'm a rusty tin can that ought to be mashed down and recycled."

Alison reached over—one of her rare gestures of affection—and patted Lucy's cheek gently. "Not you. I didn't mean you. You'll never be a resigned old woman. You'll reach out and grab at life as long as you can breathe. I feel better just being around you. Maybe it's Hollywood that's got me down. It's macabre now, like an abandoned stage set of a boom town. Even the top people are panting to make TV commercials so they'll collect residuals." She hissed the *sid*. "Thank God I salted away my money so I don't have to play old Granny gulping a laxative before the little beasts come to visit."

Lucy soon showed signs of the restiveness she was apt to feel when the subject of the conversation wasn't herself. Alison, noticing the signals, said, "And I'm glad Hal left you so nicely fixed you don't have to scrounge around illustrating for *Poultry Gazette*."

26

Lucy, like her husband, had been a well-known magazine illustrator. *Poultry Gazette*, indeed! She said stiffly, "The Wingate Gallery can never get enough of my watercolors." This was a slight exaggeration. In the summer months, sales were fairly good; in winter, even Santa Claus didn't help.

"Does your inspector have money? Tell me about him. When you wrote that you'd rented Hal's old studio to him, I knew he must be really special."

"He's not *my* inspector. I only rented the studio because I needed the money." This last sounded rather unconvincing, even to Lucy. "I'll have to find another tenant any day now because McDougal's going back to his wife. Or ex-wife. She's flying in from Europe today. Her second husband's much younger, and I suppose he got tired of her so she's snatching Mac back." It was meant to sound like a casual you-know-how-those-things-happen remark, but there was an undertone—or undertow—of deep-running hurt and resentment.

"Lucy!" Alison flung out one hand, and her voice became throatily throbbing. "My dear, I'm so sorry. But of course at your age. . . ."

The jab put Lucy, belatedly, on guard. She became even airier. "Oh, it doesn't affect *me*. There's never been anything between us. Mac's the one to be sorry for. The wife made a fool of him by having an affair right under his nose. The man was some arty type who was hired to direct a little theater group in Hartford. He was a disciple of Polanski, whoever *that* is." Lucy's tone consigned Polanski to some piddling nether region reserved for nonentities. "The Theatah of Participation. And Mac's wife went for participation, lock, stock, and mattress. Mac was head of the Connecticut State Police, homicide division, and he found out about it from one of his own detectives."

"If he was head of homicide, he could have got away with murder. *Crime passionnel.* The French do those things so much better."

"Oh, Mac wouldn't kill anybody. The wolf can gnaw at his vitals and he won't even utter."

"You mean fox."

"Wolf is more suitable—considering the man who made love to Mac's wife. Of course it was terribly humiliating, but he shouldn't have taken it lying down."

"Sounds to me as if his wife did all the lying down."

Lucy detested being interrupted, except by herself, and now that she'd got on the subject of McDougal, she felt a compulsion to talk. She ran her hands through her short, curly white hair till it stood out like a Hottentot halo. "Will you shut up and let me finish? McDougal retired from his job as soon as he found out, and he came down to Wingate and just burrowed into some dark little motel room to suffer. Talk about recluse—when I met him he was like an ossified clam."

"Anybody who wanted to be a recluse should never have rented a studio on your place."

"I know." Lucy's voice was creamy with self-satisfaction. "I've been good for him. And I've helped him a lot with his work."

"I thought you said he'd retired."

"Except when we get a good murder. The local police are terribly shorthanded. Especially now that more women are taking to crime. I think it has something to do with Women's Lib. Anyway, the police like having an inspector on tap."

"So he and the ex-wife will remarry and live around Wingate."

"I haven't the foggiest notion where they'll live. But Mac loves this part of Connecticut." Lucy's shoulders, usually so straight, hunched tiredly. "I think I'll sell my house and get an apartment in some decent climate. It's too much for me to handle alone." She wouldn't add, even to herself, *With Mac gone.* Instead, she said, too quickly, "I've been thinking about it for several years."

She stared out through the French doors at the rolling green lawn McDougal had worked on so doggedly, against moles and drought and dandelion thistles blowing like tumbleweed. The Oriental poppies were blazingly beautiful right now. Even the white lilacs were almost as lush as the purple this year; Mac was a demon for fertilizer. Good thing he'd set out the plants in the cutting garden last weekend. What was that rabbit-repellent stuff he'd used on the marigolds? She could see his lanky figure bent over like a croquet wicket while he sprayed the tiny new plants. Magic Circle, that was it. Even the name seemed a mockery now.

"This is the time of year to start showing the place, while everything looks so—" She started to say *beautiful,* but the word lumped in her throat. "I'll call the real estate people Monday."

"Then we'll have to live it up this weekend." Alison was gamely acting Vivacious Guest. "What are you going to wear to Larry's?"

"If you won't go, I won't either." Lucy was acting Thoughtful Hostess, but the line came across as more of a bleat from a lamb to be sacrificed.

"Of course I'm going. Now that you've told me Larry's a teetotaler convalescent with a keeper, I wouldn't miss seeing how miserable he is."

Lucy revived so fast she forgot her original story

of "quiet little evening." "Larry said he'd ask Doug Brill. Doug's just back from Spain."

"Are they speaking again?"

Lucy looked baffled.

"Don't you remember the great brouhaha when Larry took over Doug's wife and made her Number Two?"

"Oh, Madeline. Of course. I always thought she was a better actress offstage than on." Alison looked gratified, so Lucy prattled on: "I remember going to a party there, and the ceiling in her bedroom was all mirrors. Imagine going to bed with *that* ego."

"Larry did more than imagine it. Maybe he was doing research for the bedroom scenes in his next book. I used to think he got his sex stuff out of an eighth-grade physiology textbook. Why anybody would ever want to ban *Wayward the World* is beyond me. So old-fashioned. Not even any oral intercourse, to speak of."

"I'm dying to hear what Larry says about the book burning."

"He's apolitical and amoral," Alison said. "Don't count on him to do anything except for himself."

She was looking broody again, and Lucy switched subjects hurriedly. "I forgot to tell you—the baby he dangled out the window will be there."

"I can't quite imagine her out of that dog basket, but she must be in her thirties now, so she's probably outgrown it." She yawned. "I need my beauty nap if I'm going to be jazzy tonight. I think I'll wear my kimono."

"To the *party?*" Lucy looked dubious.

"Well, it's called a caftan or something. Black with red dragons shooting flames. What's a forked tongue? Did you ever see one?"

"Only yours." She hadn't meant to say it, and she laughed to show she hadn't meant it—much.

When they went upstairs, Lucy had a girlish longing to show Alison the dinner dress she was going to wear that night: white spattered with violety-blue flowers. Alison, between cavernous yawns, said "Charming," slurring the *r* so it sounded too Britishly polite.

Lucy carried the dress back from the guest room to her own room, fuming, then posed before the long mirror, holding it up with the hanger tucked under her chin. The sight was balm to her prickled vanity; the flowers were the same blue as her eyes.

She slathered her face with a new cream that bragged on the label that it contained turtle hormones and buttermilk. Perhaps it was this combination, on top of the lobster salad for lunch, that made her nap so unrestful. She dreamed she was in front of Coleman's Market, on Main Street, when Inspector McDougal came out of the police station opposite and beckoned to her urgently. But she couldn't get across to meet him because traffic rolled in a relentless stream, computerized green forever.

Inspector James McDougal, driving his Buick down the Saw Mill River Parkway, was in the manic-depressive state of a bridegroom who doesn't like brinkmanship. His driving, usually so sane and sensible, reflected the shifts from wild elation to gray foreboding: spurts up to an illegal seventy-five to pass a car, then veering into the slow lane to brood. Eileen had said on the phone from Warsaw it had been all her fault, before. "Oh, Mac, if you knew how bitterly I've blamed myself. You were my anchor, and I'm so adrift. I need you." Even hearing her voice so unexpectedly in the night had set off waves of physical longing. "I want you."

He had wanted her too. All the more when she asked so humbly if he'd take her back. He knew from her voice she'd been crying. She had always cried like a child—suddenly, stormily, never swollen red eyes. As a cop, he had seen a good many women cry, and their tears made him uncomfortable. But Eileen's crying had always dissolved him, as if her tears flooded his heart and carried off residue anger. In the two years since she'd been gone, he'd had recurring nightmares, even wide awake, of Eileen alone in some foreign city, abandoned by her new husband, or sick and longing for home. She'd always been compulsively propelled, like a shooting star that can't help it. Whirling from enthusiasm to enthusiasm: the last year of their marriage it had been something called Tactile Consciousness, and then the Theatre of Participation, and then— But he'd left her alone too many nights. She'd complained he never wanted to go anywhere unless there was an interesting corpse. Now that I'm retired, I'll have time to go with her, share things with her. We can travel whenever she likes. First, we'll stay in New York awhile and see some shows and go to a nightclub or two. . . .

Even the thought of going to a nightclub made his palms feel clammy on the wheel. He'd have time to take a shower at the hotel before he went out to Kennedy to meet her plane. And he'd get his unpacking over with. Eileen had once described to a friend gaily, in his hearing, how Mac had behaved on their honeymoon. "The minute we got into our hotel room, the first night, Mac had to unpack. He put things in bureau drawers in neat little piles—shorts here, handkerchiefs there, shirts in virginal packets. It all had

32

to be just so before he'd make love." McDougal had been angry and hurt. For days afterward, whenever he undressed in their bedroom, he'd tried to throw his clothes around to show how unfettered he was, like his beautiful wife. But the messiness made him so uncomfortable he soon had to revert. A month or so later, Eileen had read him a passage from *Winesburg, Ohio* in which the young George Willard had suddenly told himself, "In every little thing there must be order, in the place where men work, in their clothes, in their thoughts. I myself must be orderly. I must learn that law. I must get myself into touch with something orderly and big that swings through the night like a star. . . . I must begin to learn something, to give and swing and work with life. . . ." Eileen had said, "That's you, Mac. But you were born knowing it. Teach me." Even her inconsistencies, however maddening, were part of her appeal. And whenever she'd carelessly hurt him, she'd always had a rushing urge to make up for it. Not just in bed, although that had been fine too, until those last months. . . .

A nervous little *toot-toot* penetrated, finally, and made him glance in the rearview mirror. The toot had come from a Saab like Lucy's, snailing along behind him. Woman driver, hunched forward to clutch the wheel, oversteering. Lucy would never be in a slow lane. She zoomed. But she was a damn good driver, except for that tendency to park near fire plugs. Sergeant Terrizi ought to give her a ticket sometime. The idea of the sergeant or anyone else on the Wingate police force daring to give Lucy a ticket split McDougal's long, lean face into a grin. Lucy made her own laws to suit the occasion, the way she cooked. Good cooks were supposed to make a mess of a kitchen, but Lucy never did. Odd, that for so whirlwind and impulsive a woman she had such an instinct for order. She was never sloppy; that was it. She lived without clutter. McDougal pulled up behind a sedan with a crumpled rear, passed it, cautiously, and thought about Lucy's big sunny kitchen. He wondered what she was cooking for dinner for the weekend guest. Some old friend from California she hadn't seen in years. It was better for her not to be alone. Maybe he could go on renting her studio, and then he and Eileen could go up for weekends. Up from where? The city? The threat of living in New York mushroomed into such an ominous cloud that he could only get out from under by concentrating on having the studio for weekends. He could still do most of the gardening that way. And Lucy would ask them often for dinner. Eileen had never really been housebroken, domestically. She had come from a wealthy family, she'd inherited money of her own, and anything to do with fixing food bored her; they'd had an erratic succession of cooks. But Eileen would enjoy Lucy's little dinner parties. She loved parties.

It occurred to McDougal, like a revelation from on high, that however different his ex-wife and his landlady were, they were astonishingly alike in several ways: both impulsive, generous, childlike, greedy for new experiences and new people, reacting like prisms to color and gaiety and light. Of course, Eileen was much younger than Lucy. And she's twelve years younger than you are, McDougal told himself, ready to poke the thought like a sore tooth. But then he remembered something Lucy had said that morning before he left: "Mac, you look at least ten years younger than when I met you. Eileen's going to see a big difference." For one thing, he'd never had time to get a tan before, not to keep. Maybe all heads of

34

homicide were doomed to be an unhealthy gray-white like the corpses they dealt with. The replay of Lucy's voice started up again. "You looked like a stilt and you walked like a stilt and you talked like one. If Eileen did that to you, don't you ever let her do it again. But don't go out to the airport wearing chips on both shoulders like epaulets. Hal would have taken me back no matter what I'd done. And if you're that way about Eileen, then you're doing the only thing you can do. But I want you to remember you're a very attractive man, and you're damn good in your field."

But what field was left? If he ever yielded to the old itch to investigate a killing and went off single-minded as a bloodhound and left Eileen alone for days or weeks. . . . No, that was out. It was good therapy when I felt like an amputee after the divorce. But now with Eileen back I won't need anything else. For a moment, he felt hollow-headed, as if he hadn't eaten for a week. Then a new idea burst like a rocket inside him. Maybe Eileen, with her eager reaching out for new experiences, would get interested in help-ing him on an occasional case. After all, look at Lucy Ramsdale. Lucy looked about as likely a criminal in-vestigator as a—he groped for a simile—butterfly? Hummingbird? Too lightweight. But anyway, Lucy had shown real flair as a neophyte detective. And Eileen might too. A deep, cool part of his mind where wishful thinking couldn't penetrate said, But that's how you met her in the first place—a Junior Leaguer interested in prison reform. Eileen never sticks at any-thing. She's never had to.

He was on the West Side Highway now, and a billboard for Scotch, Chivas Regal, loomed as a wel-come distraction. That was Eileen's brand. He'd pick up a bottle right after he left the car in the 58th Street garage. They could have a drink or two in their room before they went out for dinner. Maybe they wouldn't go out for dinner. They could have something sent up later. In the old days he had never wanted a bellhop or waiter, or even a maid, to come into a hotel room and find them both in bed. He had always grabbed his robe or, better yet, his pants, if there was time, and stood stiffly, seemingly detached, as if the rumpled bed had nothing to do with him or he with it. Eileen never gave a damn what people thought, and she'd been amused by his fierce sense or privacy, or what she called his ex-Presbyterian morality. Once she'd said, "Would you like me to wave my wedding ring around? Or wear it through my nose, to show we're legit?"

It came to him now, with a spurt of astonishment, that they wouldn't be legit. She'd have to get her divorce first. Maybe he should have reserved adjoining rooms. Maybe he could still change the reservation he'd made on the phone. The Plaza was Eileen's choice. Her family had always stayed there when they came to New York. McDougal had never felt quite comfortable at the Plaza. It wasn't just that it was too rich for his Scots blood; it gave him a sense of being gawky, out of place, like a guest who'd wandered into the wrong party.

He had the same feeling but intensified, a half hour later, when he went up the steps to the Plaza, carrying his bag in one hand and clutching the package of Scotch in the other. In the lobby, he hesitated. If he changed to adjoining rooms, should he reserve one in Eileen's current married name? He was damned if he would. Exhilarated by this defiance of law and order, he strode to the desk. "I have a reservation for a double room. James McDougal."

"Inspector McDougal?" the reservations clerk said respectfully. Why, he was known. He hadn't used his title when he phoned. But his picture had been in the *Times* and on television the summer before when he'd worked on the second murder case in Wingate. . . . For once, McDougal's fierce sense of privacy didn't hackle; it was pleasant to be recognized at the Plaza —at Eileen's hotel.

"Yes, I'm Inspector McDougal," he said, not curtly at all. He was in such a good humor he came near making a small joke about it: Would you like to see my police credentials? But that was more chit-chat than he could manage.

"I believe we have an urgent message for you, Inspector. If you'll just sign the register, while I check on that. . . ."

# 3

Jeff Solent, teacher of Drama and Film Studies at Wingate High School, was lolling on the bed haranguing his girl while she tried to hook herself into a strapless bra. "You're politically and emotionally immature. It isn't the books being destroyed that burns you. All you're really dithering about is Dilman's *Wayward the World.*"

Marcy Coving completed the hooking and took a trial breath to see if the structure would hold; it held very staunchly. She untied her long hank of hair, picked up a brush from the dressing table, and began to stroke vigorously.

"I believe in the freedom to read," she said, stroking with her head upside down.

"You say that like a parrot. It's something you learned in library school, and you've been mouthing it ever since. But I don't see you running to Eldridge Cleaver to apologize for his book being banned."

Marcy came popping right side up. "He's in Algeria."

"That's beside the point. Even if he were here in Wingate—"

"He'd still be a fugitive from justice."

"Or injustice. But you wouldn't be running to him to apologize."

"I am not running to anyone." She shook her pale yellow hair, now floating silkily free. "And I care about *any* author's book being banned. But it just happens Mr. Dilman is the only one I could phone and apologize to personally." There was a defensive note in her voice. "He couldn't have been sweeter."

"You sound sexy on the phone."

"Don't be disgusting. Lawrence Dilman wrote that book before I was even born. And he's been terribly sick." She carefully didn't add that she had expected to hear a quavering old voice on the phone and had been surprised and charmed to hear something quite different. The famous author had not only sounded virile; when she'd asked, nervously, if they might use his name as honorary chairman of a committee to defend the books, he had said, "Honorary, hell. I'll make that woman back down if I have to throttle her myself." He had asked her to come have a drink, and by then he was sounding a bit too cozy: ". . . guests for dinner later, but if you come at five, you and I can get off by ourselves and get to know each other." It had made her slightly cautious. Now, as she took her least bookish dress out of the closet, she said, "I told Mr. Dilman I had a date, and he very graciously asked me to bring you along."

"'Graciously,'" he mimicked. "You're a product of women's magazines. 'How to serve hogwash graciously when your husband's boss is coming to dinner.'"

"You keep knocking marriage, but I notice you want everything that goes with it. You won't let me see anybody else and you criticize the way I do breaded pork chops and you try to force your opinions on me and—"

"Well, there's one thing I don't force on you." Under the large and straggly moustache, he was grinning. "Sexually, you're mature, my little chickadee."

"Don't you quote W. C. Fields at me," she said furiously. "You drag me into New York to see silly old movies and you make me sit up half the night watching Carole Lombard or Marie Dressler on the Late Show— Which reminds me, last Sunday you left your car parked in front of my apartment all night. I've told you and told you—"

"That was nothing I'd planned. Remember? You said you'd send me home early because you had to wash your hair and read *Wilson's Library Bulletin*. And then you lured me into helping you wash your hair—"

"You insisted. You wouldn't even leave till—"

"A male should share difficult chores. The first commandment of Women's Lib. And as a reward for my helpfulness I got sopping wet. I also got something called Protein Thirteen, which is the consistency of raw white of egg, down my neck—down . . . down . . . down . . . ."

He was making gestures which might have been construed as matey, but his companion was absorbed in putting on a lipstick called Lotus Lick.

" . . . so naturally I had to get out of my clothes. And I couldn't very well run out naked at three A.M. and move the car." He added virtuously, "That would have caused talk."

"It's caused plenty of talk already, leaving your car there. The woman across the street snubbed me in the A & P. She looked right through me."

"Sex-starved biddy. I refuse to let my life be run by a bunch of unlaid hens." He sat up and thumped the pillow. "What do we think we're in, President McKinley's New Frontier?"

"It's easy for you to take chances. They won't fire you—you Yale cum laude. But I graduated from a school nobody ever heard of, and this is my first job, and I'm already in enough of a mess. And Con-Com's no help." Superintendent of Schools Bolling, who had been appointed by the school board the year before. talked fulsomely in meetings about "finding an agreeable compromise" and had been dubbed by dissident members of his staff The Connecticut Compromise—Con-Com for short. "He told me not to replace the books till the school board votes on it. And you know how they'll vote—six to three against. That's how they got rid of the ethnic studies course."

"But they can't let a nut who's not even a member of the board get away with destroying school property."

"This nut happens to have given the new athletic field. Or her husband did."

"She probably chopped up the books with Hampter Honing Razor Blades so they'd burn easier."

"Con-Com hinted that she's threatened to withhold the rest of the endowment—for the upkeep of the field—if the books are replaced."

"Let her keep the money to wipe her backside."

"And ask the taxpayers to shell out again? They already voted down the last two raises in school taxes."

"If the school board goes along with Hampter, I'll report it to the CTA. Then the teachers will walk out. Most of them are on your side."

"They can't afford to leave their jobs any more

than I can. It's already May. Do you know how many applications they had here for five vacancies next fall? Four hundred and seventy-nine. Con-Com's secretary told me." She yanked her dress over her head and shook it down in a pragmatic shimmy. "So who's going to storm the Bastille?"

"Students. The seniors are getting up a petition."

"And by next week it will be a petition to legalize grass before the Senior Prom."

"That kind of cheap cynicism doesn't sound like you." He grinned suddenly. "It sounds more like me."

"It didn't come cheap. I was conned by a student," she said, with bitterness. "I let myself in for this mess."

"Hang loose, kid. You can always get some sort of job."

She flung her hair back and her nostrils dilated—in and out like a bellows. "It's simple for you to talk," she began. "You don't send money home every two weeks...."

He could see what was coming, the "spoiled only child—Picasso in the bathroom" attack.

He had taken Marcy Coving down to New York to spend Easter weekend with his parents in their comfortable ten-room cooperative apartment, and he had thought the visit was a smashing success all around. But the next time Marcy got sore at him, she had said furiously, "It's all very well for you, a spoiled only child. *Your* family has a Picasso in the bathroom. Do you know what my family has? A dollar-ninety-eight reproduction of Monet's Boy with Fife."

He had said, "Much more suitable for a bathroom," but this had only made things worse, because Boy with Fife, it turned out, was in the Covings' living room, featured over the mantel. He had tried to recoup by pointing out that the Picasso was only a drawing, but for some reason this hadn't gone down well either.

"It's all very well for you to make splendid gestures," Marcy said now, in an ominous tone.

To forestall the Picasso-in-the-bathroom diatribe, he said quickly, "Do you realize it's almost five o'clock?"

"Oh, my lord. You ought to put on a jacket."

"You're dressing for two." He rolled back again, all six feet one of him, in chino pants, checkerboard shirt, and bare feet. He had nice, long lean feet with straight toes.

The only house rule he observed meticulously was: "Don't get on my bed with your shoes on." This was Marcy's first apartment, and she was as fussy as an old bachelor. The tiny place resembled a series of Chinese boxes—living room, kitchen, bedroom—that would fit inside each other and store in a closet.

"I'll put on my shoes and walk softly and be meek when the great lion roars." He swung around to put his feet on the floor and reached down for his sneakers.

"Do I look all right?" Marcy had turned from the mirror, and she sounded very young and anxious. Considering that she was wearing a halter-topped, abbreviated white dress that left perhaps two thirds of her splendidly curving self bare, it was a somewhat incongruous question.

"You'll do." If it was meant to sound tough, Humphrey Bogartish, the doting note still seeped through.

"You don't think I'm overdressed, do you?"

43

Jeff stopped tying his left sneaker to take an appreciative look. Then he fingered his moustache like a villain in an old silent movie. "Not for me. But for a sick old crock like Lawrence Dilman—baby, you're dressed to kill."

# 4

Georgina Hampter had descended on Ronnie Ellis's mother and they were having a showdown in the Ellis living room, which had plastic dust covers on the lampshades and smelled of furniture polish. The curtains—Mrs. Ellis called them "drapes"—were drawn to protect the royal blue carpet from fading in the afternoon sun.

Life had already faded Mrs. Ellis to a grayish-yellow tone; she looked as if she were made mostly of chicken bones.

Georgina Hampter was a tall woman of fifty, with a figure meant to be ample but rigidly controlled by diet and custom-made corsets, and fair skin and blond hair expensively tended. Lucy Ramsdale had once described her as "curdled peaches and cream," and in some odd way this caught the essence of Georgina. Under that tightened exterior, occasionally one could get a glimpse of a naïve country girl who had been poured into the wrong mold to set and sour there.

"You told me Ronnie wouldn't get into any trouble for taking out the books on his card. And now they're trying to suspend him." Mrs. Ellis's shrill voice had a snuffle in it.

"If he'd stuck to his story, nobody could have proved he didn't lose the books."

"I told you, the librarian smelled something funny and—"

"Naturally she smelled something funny when the only book Ronnie returned was the Reverend Willy Gresham's *Minus Is Plus*. I put that on the list to make the whole thing look noncontroversial."

"Well, I saw no call to pay good money for a book we wanted to keep in the library."

"It was *my* money. And if you'd done as I told you and waited to send in the check until after school was closed for the summer, then we'd have had time to get all the signatures we need."

"The books was due," Mrs. Ellis said sullenly. "And the librarian called Ronnie into her office and kept asking all those questions."

"All he had to do was keep his head." Georgina might have added, If he ever had one, but there were times when even she had to temper her sails to the wind—this time, the gale-force winds of a furious mother. "He didn't have to involve me at all."

"Why should he take all the blame? It was your idea in the first place."

"You've complained often enough about the filth that's taught in the schools."

"The police could have taken care of it. They've been cracking down on pornography."

Georgina's lips twisted. "Pornography in a newsstand. But what good does that do when they can get it from a library—*free?* I talked to Chief Salter myself, and he said it was up to the school board. But the school board hasn't the guts. If I'd been a member—"

"Well, you aren't. And you had no right getting Ronnie to do your dirty work."

Georgina was so incensed that rays seemed to shoot from her head, as in a comic strip. "Dirty work! Protecting young people from filth!"

"They aren't so young as all that," Mrs. Ellis muttered. "My Tom used to say if they don't get it one place they'll get it another."

"Your husband was the last person to set any moral standard. A common drunk."

"You've got no right to speak ill of the dead. If he'd still been alive, he wouldn't have let Ronnie get into this mess."

"Ronnie is not in a mess. We'll have our meeting of Concerned Citizens Monday, and we'll get enough support to make sure the books aren't replaced in the library. Ronnie will end up a hero, a clean-cut young athlete who's helping to fight pornography."

"That's not how they're talking at school. Even some of the kids on the track team are treating Ronnie like he was a stool pigeon or something. And that Coving girl, the librarian—she called Ronnie a contemptible sneak. He was real upset."

"Marcia Coving is not fit to have contact with young people. She and that drama teacher are totally immoral."

Mrs. Ellis's squinty little eyes glistened. "How do you know?"

Georgina gave the pleasurable sigh that precedes a feast of tittle-tattle.

# 5

Alison had insisted on calling the nearest limousine-for-hire place and renting a car and driver for the evening. "I refuse to crunch myself and my kimono into that bug of yours," she told Lucy. "We'll make our entrance in style. Remind me to get a good entrance line."

In an outsize way, Alison was looking quite spectacular: crimson dragons writhing on the tent-size black garment, gray hair piled high and held with a jeweled comb, a bracelet clanking with elaborate gold charms, including a jeweled bird in a cage. The Cadillac limousine and uniformed chauffeur seemed modest, even bourgeois, in contrast.

When this hired conveyance brought them up the long curve of driveway to the many-pillared, twentieth-century Colonial house, the only other car parked in front was a muddy little green Karmann Ghia with a bashed left fender. There was also one motorbike.

Alison, inspecting them through an invisible lorgnette, oozed satisfaction. She slid into her gracious-lady role, deliciously contralto, giving instructions to the driver about picking them up. "Mr. Dilman, our host, has been very ill and he's on an invalid schedule, so we'll want to leave early . . ."

It reminded Lucy of a *grande dame* who had come calling soon after she and Hal moved to the country and had given gracious advice about how to treat servants. "When you give them instructions, always take them into your confidence as to *why* you want something done. Then they feel you're their friend and they'll stay with you forever." But within a few years, her staff had deserted to work in the new factory, and the white elephant of a house had finally been sold to an undertaker.

". . . so shall we say ten fifteen?" Alison was saying.

Lucy had got out of the car first and was facing Alison as she billowed her way out, looking as if she'd come in costume to open the fete for a worthy charity. Alison's expression changed so abruptly that Lucy turned to see what had caused it. Larry Dilman was coming across the lawn to meet them, looking very fit and flat-stomached in a Madras jacket, holding a glass in one hand and pulling along a pretty young floating-haired blonde with the other.

Alison muttered, "You and your 'limp vegetable left out in the sun too long!' I could kill you."

"He must have had an injection of goat glands since I saw him." Lucy said it out of the side of her mouth; her smile had been frozen into place at the sight of Larry. He did look rejuvenated.

"And the wife. I suppose a fairy godmother waved a wand and said, 'Away with that thick-ankled technician look.'"

"That's not his wife. It must be the daughter."

"Has he added incest to his repertoire?"

"Alison Moffat! It's great to see you."

Alison extended her hand, limp-wristed. "Larry, how nice."

Their host let go of the girl to take the hand, but he didn't let go of the glass, which tilted and sloshed a bit of his drink onto Alison. She managed almost simultaneously to shake herself and her dragons disdainfully, smile with warm insincerity, and, while Larry was greeting Lucy, say to the blonde, "My dear, I knew you when he dangled you out the window in a dog basket."

The girl looked rather alarmed and moved closer to Larry, who took her hand again.

"They think you're my daughter. That's a good idea—I'll adopt you, Marcy Coving." He introduced Alison and Lucy. "Two very old friends. They knew me when I was writing *Wayward the World*."

The girl exhaled *oh-h-h* in a reverent way. "Isn't it a beautiful book? I've been terribly upset about what happened at school. It was really my fault. Mr. Dilman's been so kind about it."

Lucy could see why he might be. Marcy Coving, in the halter-top, miniskirted white dress, was enough to inspire kindness, not to mention more earthy emotions.

Alison rattled her charm bracelet imperiously. "You're the student who took out the books for that witch."

"Oh, *no!*" It was a cry of real horror. "I'm the librarian."

"You should go on *What's My Line*. They'd never guess. The old stereotyped images die hard. Larry, I want to sit down and I want a martini. I spent enough years talking on my feet."

She started toward the front door, but Larry veered her on a fresh course. "Bar's set up on the terrace." The brick walk leading around to the side of the house was too narrow for him to accompany Alison. As she went down the walk with Larry just behind her, Lucy, trailing with the girl, heard him say, "Do you know the last time I saw you, Alison? When I was in the hospital after my heart attack. The nurse came in and woke me before six and put on the TV and there you were on the Late Late Late Show just ending . . ."

"She's a movie actress?" the girl whispered to Lucy, who nodded, wanting to go on eavesdropping. "Jeff— the friend I'm with—will be terribly interested."

". . . so I had seven minutes of feasting on that dearly loved face of long, long ago."

Lucy, listening to the mocking voice, thought uneasily, He's baiting her. She'll charge any minute and gore him.

It was done somewhat more bloodlessly, after the women had settled down and Larry was standing at the glass-topped table set up as an impromptu bar.

Alison didn't have to raise her voice; it carried like a guided missile.

"Larry, I heard you'd married a nurse or something. It must be such a comfort to be well looked after in your declining years."

Her victim lifted his chin so that the crepiness in his neck didn't show as much. It was still a good profile, although his lower lip was too full. His hair was white and thick, worn rather long and boyishly rumpled; the eyebrows were still dark, and went up in a triangle, so that they gave his face a slightly Mephistophelian air. "You'll be sorry to hear I never felt better in my life." He glanced meaningfully at Marcy Coving. "Having a book banned is the best thing that's happened to me in years."

"Where's your wife?"

"In the kitchen diddling with lamb for shish

kebab. And Joan, my daughter, is tending the sacred flame back there." He waved a hand toward a spot a hundred yards away, where several people were grouped around an outdoor fireplace. "We're having a cookout." His voice put fastidious quotation marks around *cookout*.

Oh, God, Lucy thought. The last time she'd been there for dinner, Larry had been between marriages and he'd had a superb cook. All day, to counter her depression, she'd kept picturing a long-stemmed-wine-goblet kind of dinner party with marvelous food and amusing people and the kind of admiration she and her dress deserved. Now all her party gaiety felt dried up inside her.

The young blonde was talking earnestly to Alison. ". . . been suspicious if all the books on the student's list were like Cleaver's *Soul on Ice,* but when I saw *Wayward the World* and *Grapes of Wrath,* I just couldn't imagine. I mean, they're *classics.*"

Larry, delivering Alison's martini, was in time to hear this, and Lucy started to wink at him to share the joke. But it wasn't a joke to the author; he looked downright fatuous. He patted Marcy Coving's silken blond head and then, more lingeringly, her bare left shoulder. "This child came over practically in tears to apologize." He went on patting the "child's" shoulder. Marcy looked uncomfortable; she shifted in her chair, disengaging, but unless she made an issue of it—"Unhand me, you cad"—there wasn't much she could do.

Lucy thought in exasperation, Alison's right. He's apolitical and amoral and he isn't going to do a damn thing to help.

She said, "Georgina Hampter will fight like a hellcat to keep those books from being replaced in the library. What are you going to do about her and her Citizens for a Clean-Minded Community?"

"We'll form Citizens for a Dirty-Minded Community," Larry said. "I hereby declare myself chairman."

"That isn't funny. All the lunatic fringe in this area will follow her lead."

"I'm not being funny, I'm serious. I've already promised Miss Coving: Georgina will recant and eat crow."

"This I'd like to see," Lucy said scathingly.

"Would you? Would you really?" Larry looked gay and mischievous. He also looked slightly drunk. "Behold Aladdin. You rub; I deliver. Madam Clean-Minded Hampter is coming over tonight."

"How nice." Alison lifted her glass and gave a malevolent look at Lucy. "Here's to our quiet little evening."

# 6

"If I'd been a girl baby named Georgina, I'd have thrown myself into the Ganges," Lucy said. She was sitting by the bar letting off steam to her host. "Why didn't somebody drown her at birth? And what in God's name made you ask her to come over here? An evening of that is simply too much."

"It won't be for more than a half hour. I'll give her a drink and take her off for a little talk."

"If you think you can reason with that woman, you're mad. Do you know what she did when we were trying to get the new abortion law passed? She brought a fetus in a jar to the meeting and raved on about 'Do you want legalized murder?' "

"Relax and let me take care of her." Larry held up a bottle of Carioca rum. "See, I still remember what you drink. Daiquiri or collins?"

"Scotch and water." It wasn't really her drink, it was Inspector McDougal's; she didn't know why she'd said it. "Ounce and a half."

Larry picked up a jigger. "If only they'd legalized abortion thirty years ago. Poor Joan. You'll see. In some ways, she's still in the fetal stage. I should never have been a father."

"You'd rather adopt young blondes after they're nicely formed and dandle them on your knee."

"Don't put it so crudely. You make me sound like an old-time sugar daddy. That's not fair and you know it." He looked down the terrace at Marcy Coving sitting talking earnestly to Alison. In profile, with the lovely line of throat and bare shoulders, she looked younger and more appealing than ever. "That girl genuinely cares about my writing. She makes me believe in myself again. I wish you could have heard her talking about *Wayward the World*. Having that book burned—it was as if she herself had been burned at the stake. I spent an hour reassuring her. That lout who brought her over just sat here glowering, till Barbara took him off to whittle sticks."

"Whittle *sticks?* Is that some new kind of emotional therapy?"

Larry laughed. "A throwback to voodoo? He probably felt as if he were carving me up while he sharpened those skewers. He didn't want to stay for dinner, but Marcy jumped at the chance when I dangled Georgina as bait."

"And how did Barbara jump?"

"Flat-footed. She's getting to be a—"

"Oh, Lucy Ramsdale. I didn't know you were here."

It was Barbara Dilman in the solid flesh. She was wearing a bosomy peasant blouse with a quilted cotton dinner skirt which made her look thick-waisted. Her brown hair was short and straight; "butternut" popped into Lucy's mind.

"We're so sorry your inspector couldn't come. I'm

afraid we'll only have Douglas Brill for you and Miss Moffat and Joan."

Lucy said drily, "We'll try not to tear him limb from limb."

"I'm one of Lucy's five dozen frustrated admirers," Larry said quickly. "And that's a marvelous dress she's wearing, by the way. But on Lucy anything would look marvelous."

It was overchurned butter and Lucy knew it. But after Barbara's smarting remark rubbed into a new wound—*I'll be an extra woman from now on*—Larry's blather was soothing. Lucy had never really approved of him and she still didn't approve of him, but reacting to flattery from an attractive man was as natural to her as breathing. She batted her lashes and gave her most ravishing smile. Larry splashed some Scotch in his glass and lifted it to her.

"Larry! You *aren't* having another. That's your third." Barbara turned to Lucy. "He's been such a good boy about not drinking, but today he's really gone overboard. Ever since the *Bugle* came out, people have kept phoning and coming—even a delegation of ministers."

"I did *not* drink with the ministers," Larry said virtuously. "Not even with the priest."

"Well, they took up Larry's nap time. He hasn't had any rest. He even went up to his old office over the garage—and he's not supposed to climb stairs now—and cleaned out files or something. And he keeps inviting more people for dinner."

"I invited exactly one extra person—Miss Coving—to stay for dinner. You were the one who invited that hippie she came with."

"But you can't separate a couple."

"I can," Larry said. "It's a specialty of the house.

But I asked Miss Coving to stay because I want her to be here when Georgina Hampter comes."

His wife was looking over at Marcy Coving, and hospitality was not the dominant expression on her face. She said absently, "Well, I'm sure there's some mistake about your book being included on that list. But some of the other books—I must say on those I have to agree with Mrs. Hampter. To give those to children at an impressionable age. . . . If I had a child in high school—"

"You don't," her husband said. "And you never will."

It was said so savagely it was as if he'd hit her. Barbara's firm, rosy face looked suddenly blotchy. But when she spoke, she sounded like a nurse dealing with a difficult patient. "Too many drinks on an empty stomach when you're overtired. You could at least make them weaker."

She picked up the silver pitcher and poured a generous slug of water into her husband's glass. Larry promptly dumped the watered Scotch on the lawn. "For fertilizer—otherwise known as you-know-what."

Lucy, who loathed scenes not of her own making, took Barbara by the arm and propelled her toward the front of the terrace. "Alison Moffat especially wanted to meet you."

"I'm sorry, I didn't even realize that was Alison Moffat. We've had so many people coming today I thought she was just another committee woman or something."

When Lucy made the introductions, Barbara said, "I was just telling Mrs. Ramsdale I didn't recognize you. But I used to love your movies when I was a child."

"I'd have recognized you," Alison purred. "You look just the way I expected. But were you ever really a child? Somehow I picture you as springing from a test tube full-grown."

Barbara showed her teeth uncertainly.

Larry, coming up behind her, snorted with laughter and saluted Alison. "My compliments to the chef."

"Speaking of chefs"—Barbara babbled—"dinner will be quite late—things have been so disorganized today—and I do hope you'll eat lots of hors d'oeuvres. Oh, Mrs. Terrizi forgot to bring them out." She went to the side door and called, "Mrs. Terrizi, may we have the appetizers out here?" She tossed the next line over her shoulder, like somebody tossing a pinch of salt to ward off bad luck. "Mrs. Terrizi's helping me out tonight, but she's inclined to be a little excitable."

Lucy, who had known Mrs. Terrizi for years, thought that was a remarkable understatement.

Larry said, "If you weren't so obsessed with health foods we'd still have a decent cook."

"And you'd have a fat tummy and a high cholesterol count. I've gotten his cholesterol count down below one eighty-five just since we were married."

"That's not the only thing you've brought down," Larry muttered.

Mrs. Terrizi created a diversion by charging out brandishing a large tray. She was built low to the ground and seemed to move in a kind of running crouch, with her white nylon uniform threatening to split as she went. Her curly black hair and black eyes gave off a crackling energy, geared to a voice of high-decibel content.

"Anyone for raw cauliflower, carrots, zucchini?" As she came to Lucy, she lowered her voice to what was meant to be a murmur—and was, relatively speaking. "Some antipasto, huh? Not like the spread we had for Nicky and Angie's party." Her son Nicky was Sergeant

Terrizi of the Wingate Police Force, and Angie was his fiancée. Their engagement party, which Larry and Inspector McDougal had gone to, had been a feast fit for Romans of the pre-Christian era.

Lucy, thinking of it now, nostalgically, greeted Mrs. Terrizi with special warmth and took a slice of raw zucchini sprinkled with paprika which she had no intention of eating.

"Wait'll you get a load of the main course," Mrs. Terrizi said. "That marinating stuff has everything in it but dried grasshoppers. Look, I gotta talk to you private. Walk toward the back, and I'll follow you like you want more of this rabbit food."

Lucy walked back toward the bar, with a feeble excuse about wanting more water in her drink. Her host, who had sat down beside Marcy, made a polite gesture of getting up to do it for her but was easily dissuaded. Mrs. Terrizi stuck the tray under various noses and whizzed to the bar. "Listen, what's wrong with the inspector? Nicky had to call him at that New York hotel this afternoon, and something's gone blooey. You know how Nicky is about the inspector—Jesus Christ should rate so good—but he won't tell his own mama what's up for fear I'll open my big mouth." Barbara was moving toward them purposefully. "Here comes Mother Nature," Mrs. Terrizi muttered. "Nicky's gonna pick me up here at ten after he delivers a lady prisoner to Bridgeport, so I'll sic you onto him and you find out what's on his mind. He's so worried about that hero of his he couldn't even eat supper. I was feeding 'em early before I come over here—my own manicotti— and Nicky didn't take more 'n one poke of a fork. Make like I didn't tell you nothing, and—"

"I know you have a great deal to do in the kitchen, Mrs. Terrizi," Barbara said, articulating with care.

"And you will remember, won't you, to make Mr. Dilman's shish kebab without tomatoes? Just leave the hors d'oeuvre tray on the table over there, and people will help themselves."

"Or they can get down on all fours and eat grass," Mrs. Terrizi said genially, winking at Lucy, who was too preoccupied to notice.

She looked at her watch—seven forty-two—and thought, How did it get to be so early? Over two hours till Nicky comes.

Barbara, who had spotted that gesture, the premature peek at a wrist watch dreaded by even far more assured hostesses, called to her husband, "Why don't you take Lucy out to see the greenhouse? I've heard she's quite a gardener."

"I've been wanting to get her alone." Larry gave what was meant to be a playful leer, but Lucy thought there was a muted appeal in the look.

"And will you stop by the fireplace on your way and tell Joan and Mr.—uh—that if they've finished sharpening the other skewers to take them to the kitchen? Mrs. Terrizi has to let them soak before we use them."

"When Georgina Hampter comes, let me know right away. I don't want her bothering poor little Marcy Coving."

Barbara's smile was stretched so tight that Lucy thought of a rubber band about to snap.

# 7

Larry's daughter didn't look like a fetus, but to Lucy, at least, she looked like a child's stick-figure drawing with Virginia Woolf's head on top. She was nearly as tall as Larry; her long neck, arms, and legs were bonily thin; and her print dress could have been dangling from a hanger for all the good it did her, or she it. But the elongated head had that quivering elegance of Virginia Woolf's: high, high forehead, deep-socketed eyes, long narrow nose, and sensitively molded upper lip. She'd been kneeling by the fieldstone hearth piling briquets into a miniature pyramid, and she scrambled up as if to shake hands with Lucy, then said, "Oh, I'm too filthy—the charcoal."

"I always manage to rub it on my face when I'm sketching," Lucy said.

"Mother still has a sketch you did of me in a basket. And I remember she took me to your studio one time after"—she glanced over at her father—"after Larry wasn't living with us. Your husband gave me some wonderful crayons. I think they must have been pastels because they were such lovely, muzzy colors. He let me make clouds and flowers on his drawing pad, and for quite a while after that I wanted to be a painter."

"'Wanting to be' is as far as Joan ever gets," Larry said.

Joan turned away abruptly, grabbed a fire tong, and began to rake the hot coals in a bed of gravel.

Lucy came out of her preoccupied state to leap to the defense of a Vulnerable. "Joan has plenty of time. You were eating rejection slips till you were over thirty —and letting Joan's mother support you."

A lanky young man in a checkerboard sport shirt and outsize moustache, who had one foot braced on the hearth while he whittled a point on a longish stick, stopped and raised his knife in grinning salute. "I'm Jeff Solent. I like your devious ways."

"If you're done with your carving," Larry said, "my wife wants you to take the skewers to the kitchen. And if you'd rather not stay for dinner—as you made very clear a while ago—then we'll only need one extra skewer."

"If Marcy stays, I stay," Jeff Solent said. His voice was unexpectedly clear and firm and un-hairy. Lucy couldn't see much of his mouth, because of the over-grown moustache, but his brown eyes were bright with a lively intelligence.

"I don't blame you a bit. You have a very pretty girl."

"And I intend to keep her." He glanced at Larry, then attacked the stick with his knife again. "Let the chips flip where they may."

The heat from the fire was so intense Lucy moved farther away and sat down at a redwood picnic table with benches on both sides. From there she could see the greenhouse and a young couple who had withdrawn from the group, as she and Larry approached, and were conferring in whispers. As they came forward, goldenly tan, both in jodhpurs and riding shirts, they could have posed for an ad: Honeymoon in Bermuda. The boy said, "Mr. Dilman, we have to be going along now. My wife and I certainly enjoyed having a chance to meet you."

"Nice of you to come. Sure you won't have another drink? Or stay for dinner and we'll whittle a few more sticks."

The boy glanced at his wife uncertainly, but she gave an unequivocal shake of her head. "Our baby-sitter has a date at eight fifteen." She shook hands all around like a well-mannered child. When she came to Lucy, she said, "We didn't see the *Bugle* till we came in from riding, but we were so upset we had to rush over and tell Mr. Dilman how we felt. We're members of the Civil Liberties Union, and we want to make sure this is reported. And we're going to organize a group of young parents to—well, our child won't be in high school till the nineteen eighties, but—"

"Nineteen eighty-four is already here," Jeff Solent said. "Dilman doesn't realize it. He acts as if Georgina Hampter is a joke that can be laughed off."

"I didn't say she was a joke. I said she must be *treated* like a joke. 'The devil—the prowde spirite—cannot endure to be mocked.' That's Thomas More, in case you don't know."

"I know enough to remember what happened to Thomas More."

"I'm not about to lose my head."

"From what I've seen, you already have."

Larry laughed. "That's different." In a surge of high spirits and three Scotches, he grabbed a skewer and playfully feinted at Solent. "En garde."

"I'm on guard—and you'd better believe it." Solent tested the point on his skewer, then suddenly lunged.

His impromptu sword touched Larry's jacket just above the middle button—and held there.

Larry stood very still, breathing heavily.

Joan let out a small, whimpering sound; the young couple stared like mesmerized rabbits.

Lucy said, "I'm bored with all this sophomoric byplay. Give those sticks to Joan to take to the kitchen —this minute—or I'm going home."

Both men handed over their weapons meekly, and Joan bolted toward the back of the house.

"Speaking of going home," the young wife said, "we must run."

They ran, literally, flinging their good-byes into the wind of their passing. A minute later, a motorbike roared down the driveway.

Larry said, "They'll miss the fun with Georgina."

A new voice—more a foghorn—said, "You call Georgina *fun.*"

"Doug Brill!" Lucy was so glad to see a new face she almost flung herself on this old acquaintance, and his long arms enfolded her in a wraparound hug. He was a dumpy man with a disproportionately large head ballooned in a fuzz of gray hair. He sniffed at her ear elaborately.

"Lucy, darling, you smell wicked. Norell?"

It wasn't Norell, it was Chanel Nineteen, but Lucy laughed flirtily and said, "You're too expert, you perfume taster."

Larry said, "Where the hell have you been? You're late."

Brill said he'd parked on the other side of the house and stopped in the greenhouse. "Wish I could steal your gardener for the friends who loaned me their house— the place is a jungle of weeds. Can't you spare him one day a week?" He grinned at Jeff Solent. "Dilman snitched my wife, so he owes me a few favors in return. My wife was—and is—an actress. But not as good as Alison Moffat. Where's Alison?"

"On the terrace. Go help yourself to a drink."

Jeff Solent said, "You mean Alison Moffat is *here?* My God, I've seen most of her movies a dozen times. Nobody else ever read a comedy line like she did."

"Don't waste this sweetness on the desert air," Brill said. "Come and tell her yourself."

For the first time, Jeff Solent seemed diffident. He looked a question at his host.

"Go ahead." Larry sounded surprisingly amiable. He picked up the knife Jeff had whittled with. "I want to show Lucy the greenhouse."

Lucy was in no mood for flower viewing. Her white pumps felt as if they'd shrunk in the heat from the fire, and this was an unaccustomed irritant. She still wore a size four shoe, and she'd always been slightly contemptuous of women whose feet hurt.

Larry had taken her arm and was moving off so fast she felt as if she were being dragged. But once inside the greenhouse, her mercurial spirits kited up again.

The early evening sun flowed like an amber spotlight on an enchanting variety of orchids in hanging baskets. A long trestle table against the right-hand wall held pots of velvety gloxinias, crimson and white Alpha geraniums, and double begonias as big as camellias.

Halfway down, on the left, a side door opened onto a breezeway connecting with the back of the house. The far end of the greenhouse had been made into a charming garden room. There were white wicker chairs with yellow and green cushions, a gardenia bush, sweet olive and Chinese fringe, several cacti in brightly lacquered wooden tubs, a cholla with wonderfully curved branches and golden blossoms, and a flowering saguaro.

Lucy settled down gratefully in a high-backed chair and put her small, tired feet up on a wicker ottoman. She had already made appreciative noises, and she was happy to loll back and look while Larry replaced the knife in a rack and then went around closing the upper glass ventilators.

In the back corner of the garden room, she spotted an enormous plant with spectacular creamy-white blossoms, and when she took in the shape of the leaves she gave a pleased *ah* of recognition. As soon as Larry came back and sat down, she rushed into an amusing (she thought) account of the time she'd had to do an illustration for a magazine story involving that very bush. "... and I looked in the encyclopedia first, but all it had was a snicky little drawing and a nasty description: 'hairy antlers adhere to the thickened stigmata.' So finally I had to trek all the way up to the Bronx Botanical Gardens to sketch one . . . acres of rosy blossoms, and a tottering attendant with a thing like a perfume atomizer . . ." She was used to being listened to with pleasure, and she went on for another half minute before she realized Larry had that sit-on-the-edge-of-the-chair look of somebody who wants to cut in.

When she paused, he said instantly, "Lucy, I had to talk to you. You saw how things were tonight. Barbara and I are all wrong for each other."

"You mean now that she's got you all well, you don't need her?"

Larry's full red lips pouted. "I grant you she took marvelous care of me when I was sick. But now it drives me up the wall. I don't want my pulse taken and my bowel movements recorded and my drinks diluted. I don't want my *life* diluted. I want to know I'm alive full strength. Being with Marcy Coving made me realize—"

"Larry, you only met her today."

"What's that got to do with it? *A coup de foudre . . .*"

Lucy's attention had been deflected by a sound she thought of vaguely as a door hinge squeaking.

". . . and Marcy feels the same way. I can tell."

Lucy applied what she hoped was a bucket of cold water. "You're at least forty years older than she is and you have a bad heart. You'd need a nuclear-powered pacemaker to cope."

Larry was as single-minded as a buzz saw. "Barbara has appointed herself my pacemaker. She ticks off every minute of my day. So much for jogging . . . so much for rest . . . two hours for work. She thinks if I'm shut in my office I'll automatically turn out so-and-so many pages a day on a book. But I can't work. I just bang on the typewriter so she won't come in: Now is the time for all good Samaritans to come to the aid of a desperate writer. I thought I was finished, dried up, and then Marcy came and talked about *Wayward the World* and my mind started leaping with ideas for the next book."

"She's an impressionable child who probably never met a well-known writer before. It was naïve of her to hand over those books to a moron student."

"But she couldn't imagine *Wayward the World* being controversial. She said she thinks of it as a classic."

"You and Steinbeck," Lucy said drily. She was thinking of a Saul Bellow line, 'The whale-like ego of the author.'

"Oh, Steinbeck was just thrown in as a blind, like

the Reverend Willy Gresham's cornpone. And the only reason Georgina was after my book was that—" He broke off.

"Was what?"

"Oh, nothing." His eyebrows peaked up mischievously. "Sometime later I may tell you how I made her agree to come over here. But I don't want Marcy to get any whiff of that now. First I stage my coup. Then I'm going to ask her to work for me as soon as school's out, cataloging my library and—"

"And cataloging Barbara? One wife withdrawn from circulation. Needs new binding."

"Barbara won't be here."

"Does Barbara know that?"

Larry gave her a rueful, rumple-haired-boyish look. "I was hoping you'd talk to her and make her see she'd be better off without me. She admires you. She'd listen."

Lucy sat up very straight and kicked the wicker ottoman aside. "Don't hand me the knife. Do your own stabbing. If you want a divorce, tell her yourself."

"I tried. One night last week. You know what she said? That I was overtired and I'd feel different after a good sleep. How would *you* like to live with somebody like Barbara?"

Lucy couldn't stop herself from making an *ugh* face.

"It's like being tangled up in a blanket till you smother. I know I sounded like a bastard today, but she affects me that—"

There was a *thud-thud-thud* along the breezeway, and Mrs. Terrizi came zooming through the side door as if she were chased by rhinoceri. "Get those dames out of my kitchen," she yelled, "or you won't have no dinner! Tellin' *me* how to make a salad . . . how to put meat on them sticks. . . . Mrs. Dilman was bringin' the Hampter dame back here to see you, but they have to stop and yak at me till I'm ready to bust their jaws."

Lucy turned to her host. "If you let Georgina come near me, I'll push her into that cactus."

# 8

After Larry went off with Mrs. Terrizi, Lucy stayed in
the greenhouse alone, fuming, regrettably devoid of
the spirit of "Surround yourself with beauty and let it
enter your soul." Her soul wasn't having any; she was in
a mood to fret and feel abused, but under the surface
fretting there was a deep sense of unease about McDougal. She was debating whether to try to reach him at
the Plaza when Mrs. Terrizi popped back in to report.

"He asks the Hampter dame if she'd like a drink
and she says, 'A glass of cold water would be dee-lish-
uss.' She says she walked over here from her house
and she's parched. She didn't sound parched when she
was soundin' off to me before. I felt like tellin' her,
'Drink a glass of that saffron oil you're wantin' me to put
in my salad.' Her and Mr. Dilman went into his study
and he shuts the door, and then I don't hear Hampter
doin' so much talkin' after that. He's tellin', she's lis-
tenin'. I was gettin' some snack tables out of the closet
in the back hall and I was flappin' my ears tryin' to
hear somethin' but Mrs. Dilman comes and starts tellin'
me where to set up the tables, and no tomato on Signor
Dilman's shish kebab. She's always gotta repeat the

same thing over five times, like it helps her clear her head. If you ask me, her hubby's gettin' a yen for that blond librarian. Make a nice change for him, if he don't get caught."

"You'd better watch what you say. That plant over there has ears under its hairy stigmata."

Mrs. Terrizi laughed. "OK, I get it—shut my big mouth. Dinner's not gonna be for another hour. I'll be lucky if I'm through by the time Nicky comes. They got two self-cleaning ovens in the kitchen, so I hafta cook outside. The meat'll be burned on one side and half raw on the other, and wobblin' all over them wooden sticks. With the price of meat now, who wants to take chances? But Mother Nature thinks it's healthier that way. Come on in the kitchen and I'll give you a snack before I throw myself on the bonfire."

The kitchen was self-consciously *House and Garden*-ish, with cooking utensils dangling in a kind of mobile and ceramic cocks crowing on windowsills. The only thing Lucy rather coveted was a five-foot-square butcher's block used as a worktable. On it was a grill pan holding half a dozen shish kebabs lined up in formation. They looked ready to be photographed in color: pinkish lamb chunks, red cherry tomatoes, green peppers, mushrooms, small pearly onions. For a further photogenic touch, there was a bunch of fresh herbs tied to an eighteen-inch stick; it looked ridiculously like the feather duster French maids once flicked in bedroom farces. Mrs. Terrizi pointed to a large crockery bowl of marinating sauce. "Want me to tell you what all's in it? That would knock off your appetite for sure. What'll you have for a snack?"

Lucy refused even a glass of milk, looked wistfully at the wall phone, and went off to find another out of ear range of Mrs. Terrizi or anybody else.

In the front hall, she hesitated at the foot of the curving staircase, which looked endlessly long and steep. The pain of arthritis clutched at her right leg fiercely, but she made herself grip the banister to start the long climb. A door opened someplace above her; Joan came out, dabbing her eyes with a handkerchief. When she saw Lucy, she thrust it into a pocket.

Lucy said she was looking for a phone. "A friend of mine's sick, and I want to find out how she—" The pronoun stuck in her throat. Why the hell do I gibber phony excuses?

Joan was pointing. "Right down there under the stairs."

Lucy settled thankfully on the small chair in the alcove, dragged the Manhattan phone book from the shelf beneath the phone table, and looked up the Plaza Hotel. While she was listening for Joan to come downstairs and go off, she glanced at a list of numbers taped to the wall: Doctor . . . Hospital . . . Fire . . . Ambulance —and then, incongruously, Organic Foods.

Joan still hadn't come down by the time she dialed. Through all the ringing, the "What is your number, please?" and the reringing, she was trying to think what excuse to make for calling when she got him. He loathed being fussed over. Tell him, "Somebody's horse got loose and is galloping all over your vegetable garden!" Ask him who to call at the state police barracks. It had happened before, but Mac had been there to take care of it.

"Good evening, Plaza Hotel."

Lucy said she wanted to speak to Inspector James McDougal.

"Just a moment, please. . . . We have no Inspector McDougal staying with us."

"He checked in this afternoon. I know he's there, because his office talked to him earlier." Sergeant Terrizi being the office.

"If you'll hold on a moment, I will inquire of the Reservations Clerk. . . . Inspector McDougal has already checked out."

"When?" It burst out of her.

"I do not have that information, madam."

"Did he leave a number where—"

But the phone clicked and went dead.

Damn, I forgot to ask if his wife checked out with him. But she's his ex-wife. They may have had separate rooms. I can't call back and say, "Did he leave with a woman who's not his wife?" Maybe McDougal had told Sergeant Terrizi where he was going. Eight twenty now. Another hour and forty minutes to wait. Stranded in this stupid place with no car.

In a fury of frustration, Lucy picked up a pencil by the phone pad and began to doodle. But the feel, the rightness of holding a pencil, gave her a sense of direction, and her instincts took over. She sketched for several minutes and then examined the result with childish satisfaction: Georgina Hampter in armored breastplate and panty girdle, holding a pitchfork over a fireplace. Her horns went up from her head like two inverted sausage curls. The tail didn't satisfy Lucy; too stubby, like an Airedale's. She erased it and was about to draw another when voices swirled at her from the back hall.

"I want you to come out on the terrace and tell that to Miss Coving." Larry.

Then a woman. It had to be Georgina, but she wasn't sounding like her Brünnhilde self: muted, almost throttled, as if she were strangling slightly. "You can tell her I withdraw my objections to the books being replaced. And I'll cancel the meeting of Concerned Citizens."

"It would sound sweeter coming directly from you, Georgie Porgie." Larry's voice wasn't teasing. It was slyly unpleasant.

Lucy heard an odd choking sound, almost a sob. "Don't make me. Let me go. You can make my excuses to Barbara. I'll go out through the kitchen."

"But I can't make your excuses to Miss Coving. Come on, Pudding 'n' pie. Pudding 'n' humble pie." He laughed. "Of course, if you can't bring yourself to apologize, the Associated Press is sending a stringer over this evening. They're doing a series on censorship across the country, and I'm sure he'd be fascinated with any background tidbits I could give him about that pillar of rectitude—pillaress? Which would you rather be called?"

"I hate you." But it wasn't said venomously. Something else, more like—

"Come on. You'll feel better once you've taken the plunge." Larry's voice was much closer now, and suddenly he and Georgina were there by the phone alcove. Lucy froze like a small animal; she didn't even turn her head or shift her eyes in their direction, as if by not looking she couldn't be looked at herself. She couldn't have explained her terror of being seen. Logically, she should have been gloating over the humiliation of an enemy, but the scene she'd overheard had sickened her.

When she started to get up, after Larry and Georgina had gone, her legs trembled and she felt so dizzy she sat down hard and leaned against the wall, making herself breathe deeply and quietly. Her heart was doing

74

the fast-motion thing she'd once described to her doctor as "offbeat." She tried to sink into a nobody-cares-if-I-live-or-die state of mind, but this was boringly unproductive. As soon as her head stopped swirling, her springy resilience triumphed.

When she got back to the terrace, she had the feeling of a theatergoer who returns after intermission to find the second act already, disconcertingly, well under way.

She had come around from the front of the house, and she took the nearest seat unobtrusively so as not to interrupt the performance. The whole scene had a stagey quality. Jeff Solent was sitting at Alison's feet —or, rather, crouched there—and Alison had her hand on his shoulder as if to keep him immobilized. Barbara Dilman sat tensed on the edge of a chair, projecting Anxious Hostess or Apprehensive Wife, or both. Georgina was standing facing Marcy Coving, with Larry just behind, and Marcy sat looking up with the lips-parted, startled-eyed air of an ingenue.

Georgina was saying, ". . . so Mr. Dilman's *Wayward the World* should never have been on the list. The student, Ronnie Ellis, misunderstood my instructions." She sounded as if she had a sore throat and each word hurt.

Larry said, "And how about the other books? You did tell me—didn't you—that you're sorry you acted so hastily in destroying them?"

Georgina swallowed painfully. She was clutching a large beige straw handbag, and she stared down at it as if it held some sort of talisman, or a map to follow through a maze.

Larry fed her the next lines. "Miss Coving has been very worried that you and your committee would try to prevent the books being replaced in the library. I've assured her there's no need to worry. That's right, isn't it?"

The "Yes" was barely audible. "I'll—I'll issue a statement next week."

"So that's all settled," Larry said gaily. "We'll all have a drink to celebrate. Marcy, come help me."

Marcy jumped up and almost ran to the bar.

"I can't stay." Georgina turned blindly, as if she weren't sure which way to escape. Barbara Dilman went to her and took her arm and began to talk urgently. Lucy could get only a few snatches: ". . . feel terrible about the way Larry— Please, you haven't seen the orchids. I want to cut you a spray. . . ."

Orchids for the vanquished, Lucy thought. But at the moment, she was oddly in sympathy with Barbara's trying to ease the humiliation of a guest. She even felt rather sorry for Georgina, who looked suddenly as if her clothes were too loose for her big frame; above the bland pink of her linen suit, her face was haggard.

As the two women went past the bar, Georgina stared straight ahead but Barbara glared at her husband, who was listening to Marcy too fondly to notice. It was obvious, even to those beyond earshot, that Marcy was expressing her joy and gratitude in girlishly unconfined terms. Larry responded by stroking her arm, and this time she didn't pull away.

Jeff Solent was watching them, scowling; his big moustache made him look even fiercer and snarlier. Alison, still with her mottled old hand on his shoulder, leaned over to say something presumably soothing, but Solent shook her off and sprang up as if she'd said "Sic 'em!" For a second, Lucy thought he was going straight for Larry, but instead he turned and hurtled across the lawn toward the fireplace.

She moved over next to Alison and said, "If only *we'd* come on a motorcycle, we could get the hell out right this minute. What did you think of the big apology scene?"

Alison's magnificent eyes blazed. "That stupid woman, being hauled in to say 'I'll never do it again.' However Larry pulled it off—and I can guess how—the whole thing stank. And now he's got Marcy licking his hand, ready to lie down and roll over. His newest fun and games."

"Larry's not just playing. He already wants a divorce." She felt no compunction of betrayal as she launched into a juicy account of the outburst in the greenhouse. She thought it would gratify Alison to hear how Wife Number Five was faring, and she was in a mood to have a good, scratchy gossip at Larry's expense. There is nothing like gossiping about somebody else's emotional mess to ease one's own pent-uppedness. And for someone as unused to frustration as Lucy, it was an overdue release. But at the end of the lively solo recital, Alison was looking so apoplectic that Lucy was sorry she'd chattered on. She said lightly, "At the first twinge of indigestion—which tonight's dinner ought to guarantee—Larry will be moaning for Barbara to come take care of him."

Alison muttered, "It had better happen soon. Jeff's wild. I'm worried about him." She sounded like a new mother whose baby is running a fever.

Lucy was amused and feeling a bit derisive. She thought of saying, "At your age—" to get even for Alison's crack about McDougal leaving, but she couldn't bring herself to do it. Alison's confiding in her about the disastrous affair with Larry, and the emptiness of waiting to die, had made her old friend seem almost nakedly vulnerable. She said, "You have more than your share of admirers tonight. That boy exploded with excitement when he heard you were here; he knows most of your movies by heart. And Doug Brill could hardly wait to see you." She looked around, surprised. "Where *is* Doug?"

"A reporter and photographer rolled in, and Doug had to hold them at bay for a while." Alison glanced across the lawn and said in a ho-ho Shakespearean tone, "Ah, yonder cometh our sage critic now, with the two strangers. I will leave you to converse." Then, in a normal voice, "Keep Doug entertained. I want to go talk to Jeff."

As she heaved up, Lucy said worriedly, "It's hot as hell by that fire. Why don't you take him to the greenhouse?"

"In my day it was called the conservat'ry," Alison said, sounding like her old self. She shook her fiery dragons, hitched up the flowing skirt, and tramped off. Lucy noticed belatedly she was wearing what looked like red leather house slippers. When Doug Brill tried to waylay her halfway across the lawn, Alison rolled on like a tank.

"What's with this instant-mix mother complex?" Doug complained to Lucy. "I've hardly had a chance to say two sentences to Alison since she and that kid got together. She might as well sign the adoption papers. Thank God you're here, anyway. Let's duck inside till this is over."

"This" was the interview going on at the other end of the terrace. The Associated Press reporter, a little man with furry sideburns, had hauled out a tape recorder and put it on the table beside Larry. The photographer, whose camera hung on him like an albatross, was ignoring the interviewee and thoughtfully assessing Marcy Coving. She was perched on a bar stool with

78

her miniskirt modestly tucked in and her pretty legs dangling. She smiled vaguely at Doug when he said something to her, but her attention was all for Larry.

Lucy went through the screen door into the living room and found Mrs. Terrizi setting up two more of the small folding tables. "Mother Nature decided it's too cool to eat outside. *Now* she tells me." Mrs. Terrizi was putting—almost slamming—forks and steak knives on the tables. "If she asks that Hampter dame to stay for dinner, I'll turn in my badge."

Lucy said Georgina had long since left.

"That's what *you* think. When I—"

"Hey, somebody, let me in." It was Doug Brill at the screen door, carrying drinks. "My cups runneth over."

Mrs. Terrizi cleared his path, and he deposited the two glasses on a coffee table in front of a sofa slip-covered in cabbage-roses chintz. "Thanks. Mrs. Dilman was looking for you—something about running out of briquets. She said there's another bag in the garage."

Mrs. Terrizi sighed noisily. "If this goes on much longer, we'll be burnin' chairs for firewood. In ten minutes I'm puttin' on that meat no matter who's interviewin' who. That reporter oughta ask me a few questions. I'd give him a juicy earful."

Once she'd gone galumphing out, Lucy took a cautious sip of her drink—not too strong, she decided—and settled back to have a chat with her old acquaintance. It didn't go quite as she'd planned.

"What's this I hear about you keeping a police inspector on the premises as a bodyguard?"

Lucy said, Of all the idiotic stories . . . that she'd had a tenant in Hal's old studio, he'd be moving out any day, and she'd have to put an ad in the *Bugle*. This boomeranged with a bang.

79

"Darling, you've got yourself a new tenant. The friends who own the house I'm in are coming back next month, and I've been looking for a place near here so I can spent part of the week out of Muggers' Paradise."

Lucy, feeling unaccountably, frantically trapped, said she might use the place herself as a studio and added something vague about letting Doug know later.

"I'd be a quiet, well-trained tenant. No speed, no dancing girls." He had big, sad brown eyes, and with his hunched shoulders and long arms he made Lucy think of a tame, aging gorilla.

Without thinking, she said, "How did you ever stand that mirrored ceiling in your bedroom when you were married to Madeline? Wasn't it terribly inhibiting?"

"I wasn't facing that way," Doug said, with dignity. "Not in what used to be called 'intimate moments.' In those days, the standard position for intercourse was accepted even by the intelligentsia."

Lucy laughed. "I never thought of Madeline as intelligentsia. Was she as stupid as she seemed?"

"She was so beautiful it rather confused the issue. I suppose if anybody had wanted to plumb her depths, it would have been like diving into a turquoise swimming pool and finding it wasn't filled. I knew better than to try." Doug stared at the opposite wall, seeing ghosts. "I loved her the way she was." He turned back to Lucy, and the big brown eyes weren't sad now; they shone with malice. "I knew how she and Larry would make out —both completely self-centered—like Narcissus shoving his double away from the pool. And now I have the fun of watching Larry's latest marriage. He'd never been sick before, you know, and he panicked and grabbed at the nursie-mama type. Now he's back in his old form, nibbling the grass on the other side of the fence. And that young librarian has a lit'ry crush. Remember Coward's *Hay Fever?* The weekend house party when everybody paired off with the wrong person? Alison played the Constance Collier part in the revival. I said in my review she was a greater comedienne than Constance."

"You were always her favorite critic." Lucy added hastily, "I don't mean just because you praised her."

"She certainly doesn't show it tonight. Somebody ought to write a song called the 'Cradle Rock Snatch.'"

"She's just being nice to a young fan." Lucy defended her friend with more spirit than conviction. "We'll have her sit with us at dinner—if we ever get food. Go take a look and see what's happening out there now." Lucy had been sipping occasionally on the second drink, and she no longer felt dizzy but she didn't feel like leaping up and dashing around. "Any signs of food?"

"Not that I can see. The photographer is about to . . ."

Lucy could see, in the glass of the French doors, the reflection of strobe lights flashing as Doug gave details in the rat-tat-tat style of a sports announcer.

"Larry now has his arm lightly around Marcy's shoulders. He is looking at her—closer—closer—while the camera angles in. . . . Barbara is out of the game. She looks as if she'd bitten into a wormy persimmon. . . . Jeff Whosis is veering this way. . . . No, he's turning back. . . . Alison has taken his arm and is giving him a pep talk in the dugout. . . . The fireflies are out in full strength. . . ." Doug's tone changed; he said bitterly, "It looks as if Dilman will make another home run. Somebody ought to press his jockstrap into wet cement."

"Marcy won't play his game. She's brighter than Madeline."

"You don't seriously think brains have anything to do with fucking?"

"They didn't help—" Lucy stopped and took a gulp of her drink. She was annoyed at Alison, but she had no intention of betraying her friend.

Doug was too intent on the performance outside to notice her slip. "As far as Marcy is concerned, Larry slew the wicked witch. He's the knight to the rescue, and he's playing it to the hilt. Solent looks like a silly kid in comparison."

"He'd better brandish his wooden sword again." She described the skirmish at the fireplace and wound up crossly, "It seems like a week ago. I'm so starved I could eat a raw parsnip."

"Barbara's doing her best. She's showing her teeth like a cannibal. I'd like to hear what she says to Larry after we leave. That should be a jolly postmortem. I think I'll hide under the bed with a tape recorder."

"You have a stronger stomach than I do."

"Where Dilman's involved—" he began savagely.

Mrs. Terrizi galloped into the living room swinging two bottles of wine like dumbbells. "Stir up the sediment! Eat in ten minutes."

Lucy went into the downstairs bedroom to repair her makeup before dinner and found Alison there, looking quite cheerful. Alison had opened the connecting door into Larry's study, and she beckoned Lucy to come see. "Look at that row of Dilman masterpieces bound in gen-u-ine leather. Doesn't it remind you of the Coppard story—the man who wanted a study lined in pigskin? You could chart the sequence of Larry's wives by the dedications in the books."

The middle drawer of the desk next to the bookcase was not quite shut, and Lucy automatically pushed it in; an open drawer affected her like a crookedly hung picture—her fingers twitched till she fixed it. "Barbara won't last long enough for a dedication. I wish I could feel sorrier for her, but it's like feeling sorry for your dentist. The one I really feel for is Joan. She was upstairs crying a while ago, and I haven't seen her since."

"Oh, she came down to . . ." Alison's voice trailed off. "She'll probably turn up for dinner. Let's go eat Mary's little lamb."

Joan not only turned up; she was claimed by a boisterous Jeff Solent, to sit with him and Alison. The three seemed to be the only ones who were having a gay time; even Joan was laughing as Alison regaled her young audience with stories of the old Hollywood.

Larry had snagged Marcy as his dinner partner and had pointedly excluded Barbara by arranging two of the little tables in front of a love seat. Doug Brill and Lucy asked Barbara to join them, humanely if unwillingly, so that she wouldn't be odd-woman-out.

The shish kebab was unexpectedly good and Lucy was relieved to be able to praise it, although a note of incredulity crept in, so that what she said sounded more like "My God! It's *good!*"

Barbara seemed cheered by this, briefly, but most of the time she gave off that enervating air of a hostess whose mind is someplace else. Doug Brill did his best; he told about panning a new play of a well-known playwright who wrote him furiously, "I showed your review to my analyst and he said *you* should be analyzed."

Barbara said, "And were you?"

Even Mrs. Terrizi, galumphing from group to group to fill wine glasses, was forebodingly noncommunicative; she served the salad at once, banging down the plates with an air of "The sooner I get out of here the better."

Lucy felt the same way. She made chitchat with Doug and tried not to look overtly at her watch. She was facing Marcy and Larry, and it gave her a glum satisfaction to see that neither of them seemed to be enjoying themselves. Marcy made spasmodic efforts at conversation—once her voice went up breathily on "and when you think that even Shakespeare was banned"—but Lucy thought the girl was feeling that disconcerting letdown of someone who's been made much of and suddenly finds herself ignored. Larry, after the first few cozy minutes of their dinner *à deux*, was no help at all. They hadn't quite finished eating when he got up unsteadily and said in a thick voice, "I think I'll go in and lie down awhile. Barbara, will you come in with me for a minute?"

Barbara led him away, and Lucy said, "She isn't saying 'I told you so.' She's exuding it."

Mrs. Terrizi brought coffee and announced the dessert course in an ominously negative fashion: "Custard with lumps of banana. Anybody wants it can wash their own dishes afterward." Lucy, Doug, and Marcy hurriedly declined. Lucy looked at her watch: ten minutes of ten. Sergeant Terrizi ought to turn up any time. Alison, who seemed in an uproariously good humor, was ordering four desserts. "One apiece for Miss Dilman and me, and two for our growing boy." She patted Jeff's arm. "He needs to keep up his strength."

Marcy got up. "Jeff, I think we should go."

"Why? Because your great god Dilman passed out? Now's when the party really gets going. More wine! A toast to our queen of comedy."

"Mrs. Dilman only got out the two bottles." To

84

make her point even more forcibly, Mrs. Terrizi grabbed up all the wine glasses and tromped back to the kitchen. There were sound effects: glasses and china slammed into the dishwasher, silver rattled and dropped higgle-piggle.

"Everybody come to Lucy's for a nightcap." Alison spread out her arms with the vast kimono sleeves flapping, so that she looked like some gigantic bird about to take off. "Our chauffeur will be here any minute."

"Another time," Lucy said. "Sorry—I'm tired." She wasn't sorry, she was raging mad: at her host and, above all, at Alison. She thought somberly, If Nicky Terrizi hasn't arrived by the time our car comes, Alison can damn well go home alone and Doug can take me later.

But it didn't work out that way.

When the hired driver appeared at the door, Joan rushed away to fetch her stepmother.

Barbara came out looking so distraught that several strands of hair snaked down her forehead. For Barbara, that was a sign of direness. She seized Lucy's hand. "Good night. Larry's not able to come see you off. Did you have a wrap?"

*Here's your hat, what's your hurry.* The guests—including a mutinous Lucy—went quietly. While Doug Brill fetched her sweater from the terrace, Lucy opened the swinging door into the kitchen to leave a message to have Nicky call her. Nobody there.

"Mrs. Terrizi's out back at the incinerator," Joan said. "I'll tell her you said good-bye."

In the car, Lucy burst out, "That was the most revolting so-called dinner party I ever lived through. And you were no help."

"Oh, I thought I was the hit of the evening," Alison said. "You're just jealous."

"Jealous! Of you and that hairy boy?"

"I grant you Jeff's not an inspector. But cops aren't really my style."

"And Larry wasn't *my* style—that molting Don Juan. How you could ever have—you saw how he acted tonight. Barbara was wild. And if she'd heard him telling me in the greenhouse—" In her mind, the click sound came again, louder. The door from the breezeway—somebody had opened it and stood there while Larry was ranting on about Marcy and how Barbara drove him up the wall. If his wife was the one who'd listened . . .

Lucy turned to tell Alison, but Alison's head lolled back against the seat and she was snoring—*whifflepooh*—with her mouth open.

Just as well. She'd have made some crack about the inspector conditioning me to imagine mysterious noises. Lucy huddled into her cashmere evening sweater as if it were an old-lady shawl.

At eleven, when the limousine made its ponderous way up Lucy's drive, its headlights shone on the house, strategically lit here and there to discourage burglars. And shone on the studio that should have been dark; there were lights there too.

# 9

Lucy was seldom aroused by bird chatter in the mornings because usually she beat the birds to it. She was one of those people who wake up sparkling and chatty, needing to make lively sounds—even sentences —and not just simple declarative sentences, but often a whole outburst triggered by something she read in the *Times.* Her husband hadn't been a morning person, but he had managed to say Mmm in the right places. And he had looked at her often across the table because she was so charming to look at.

That Saturday morning after the Dilman dinner, Lucy woke up even earlier than usual, feeling super-charged. It wasn't precisely happiness she felt, although that too entered in; it was more a surging sense of purpose: Inspector McDougal must be pulled out of the slump.

She had phoned her tenant the night before, right after Alison had gone to bed. "It did me good to see the lights on in the studio. I'm glad you're home."

There had been a long pause, and Lucy, who generally regarded a pause as a vacuum that required rushing into, had had the sense to keep quiet. Finally, McDougal had said, "Thanks," in so exhausted, so uncertain a voice it sounded like a patient trying to talk just after a bad operation.

"If you need anything for breakfast, let me know. My guest sleeps till noon."

At that stage, it was the most she dared do: to say, in effect, I'll be alone all morning if you want to talk.

McDougal had said, "Thanks," again, but this time with some slight strength in his voice.

Now, at dawn, Lucy's mind rode off in all directions, exploring the possible avenues to her goal. Fix a good big breakfast and take it to him around seven thirty? But if he was as sunk as he sounded, he'd hate anybody barging in. He'd take the tray, slam the door, and go back to brooding while the eggs congealed. Go work in the garden and dig up some problem that would galvanize him into action? McDougal had a special thing against cutworms, and for the first time in her gardening life, Lucy hoped the cutworms were out in good appetite. If necessary, she could break off some marigold plants in a ragged way, so that they'd look chewed. But if a man had just had his life broken in two—and Lucy was certain that the ex-wife had somehow broken him again—then chewed marigold plants were admittedly small stuff. She longed to be able to hand him something so fresh and graspable, so fascinating, that he'd have to rise to the bait. A good, provocative murder case was what came instantly to mind, but although she was an impetuous woman, and enormously resourceful, she couldn't produce a victim.

The only people she'd ever actively prayed to have dead were Hitler and Joe McCarthy, and offhand she couldn't think of anyone in Wingate she could, in all conscience, ask God to have bumped off. She never went to church, but she had her own personal brand of religion. God was God in name only, not the old Jehovah in a tatty beard but somebody kind and enormously influential who had a far from perfect batting average but often came through in the crunch. Lucy also had her own code of ethics on what should and shouldn't be prayed for. Never money or, in the old days, a fat commission to illustrate a magazine story or do a cover. And she had never prayed for wisdom or strength, because she mostly thought of herself as both wise and strong. If she flagged occasionally, she was sure she could manage the recouping of these virtues by herself. Her prayers weren't humble; they were more apt to sound a bit bossy.

As she tied the belt on her long white nylon lace robe, she said aloud, "Tell me what the hell to do for Mac."

From the kitchen window she could see the studio and the gravel parking space beside it. When she looked out soon after telling Him what to do, she was miffed to see Sergeant Terrizi's old Pontiac parked beside McDougal's Buick. She had *not* asked Him to let Sergeant Terrizi be the chief recovery factor, or even the main confidant, for the inspector. Nicky Terrizi had been her yard boy when he was fourteen, with perpetually dirty hands and a miraculously green thumb. Lucy still had a tendency to regard the sergeant as someone to order around and then reward with milk and home-baked brownies.

The sergeant, in turn, regarded Lucy with a gamut of emotions, ranging from A for Admiring to X for Xantippe.

At that moment he was saying to the inspector, "Mrs. Ramsdale was there for dinner, so it might be a good idea to ask her. This Dilman had a bad heart, and it could be he died of a heart attack, but the bellyache and convulsions—it kinda doesn't add up right. Dilman's doctor won't sign the certificate. He wants an autopsy first. The wife says Dilman had been going too hard all yesterday. She keeps saying, 'If Larry had only listened to me.' "

The sergeant was thinking wistfully along that same line himself: If only the inspector would listen to me.

Terrizi himself hadn't been to bed all night, but McDougal looked as if he hadn't slept in a week. His eyes were bloodshot and oddly glazed. He was dressed in a shirt and pants, but not the way a man dresses when he gets up on a Saturday morning in the country. Pants of a dark gray suit; long-sleeved white broadcloth shirt. No tie, but the effect was still definitely city clothes.

Terrizi had seen the inspector unshaved a few times before, when they'd been working nonstop on a case, but this time was worryingly different. Terrizi had smelled whiskey when the inspector let him in. The tall, straight-shouldered man had seemed somehow shambling, and he talked too slowly and blurrily. Not that he'd said much. "Want coffee?" And he'd got out the Chemex pot and filters, and put on the teakettle, all in slow motion, while Terrizi stood in the doorway of the little kitchen giving a rundown of what had gone on in the last eight hours. Like McDougal, the twenty-four-year-old sergeant showed signs of a rough night. His olive-green summer uniform was so rumpled it would never have passed inspection by his mother; she'd have ordered him to strip on sight. His terra-cotta coloring was muted. Only his curly black hair seemed as exuberantly unrestrained as ever.

"... I was there right after Mrs. Dilman called the

ambulance. Her husband had got much worse while she was out saying good-bye to Mrs. Ramsdale and the other lady. Dilman had been vomiting before, but she said he'd been drinking a lot when he wasn't used to it. Mama heard him say it was the shish kebabs and that burned her plenty."

Mrs. Terrizi had spilled out her grievances to her son in the Dilman kitchen and added a few dark hints of her own. Even allowing for her inflamed imagination, there had been enough odd bits and pieces to make her son decide to go along to the hospital "and keep my ears loose around all those women."

The inspector should have said, "What women?" but when he didn't, Terrizi went on as if his mentor had asked the right question.

"Dilman's wife and daughter, and for a while the school librarian was there too."

That brought a flicker of surprise. "What the hell does the school librarian have to do with it?"

Terrizi explained about Dilman's *Wayward the World* and the other books being destroyed. He was tempted to throw in a description of the librarian, but he had the Italian gift of empathy, and he sensed that the inspector would be more apt to listen, right now, if the "librarian" remained bonily impersonal, an image with steel-rimmed spectacles. It was rather like referring to Helen of Troy as "a housewife named Helen," but the sergeant knew instinctively that this wasn't the moment to throw in any sexy curves. The book banning was a good thing to stress, because he knew the inspector's views on censorship and because it tied to what he had already decided was the most peculiar part of the evening's events as he'd gleaned them from his mother:

"Georgina Hampter came over to the Dilmans' last

night and apologized to the librarian, talkin' like pebbles would melt in her mouth. Mama says it was like Dilman told Mrs. Hampter what to say and she had to say it."

Again he paused, hopefully, and this time the inspector reacted. "From what I've heard of Georgina Hampter, I can't imagine her doing what Dilman told her to do unless . . ." He relapsed into silence. Not a silence that promised results, Terrizi thought, but more as if the inspector had wandered off and stepped into a bog.

"Unless Dilman had something on her," he prompted, almost pleadingly. "That's what I thought too."

The teakettle screeched, but the inspector only looked at it vaguely. Terrizi measured out two scoopfuls of Brown and Gold coffee, dumped them into the Chemex filter, and poured the water through slowly, as he'd seen McDougal do. He got out cups—big cups. Then he carried the tray into the studio's huge main room, which soared up two stories to the skylight. He thought suddenly, with a pang, of the first time the inspector had seen this room, when they had come to interview Lucy Ramsdale after a murder.* McDougal had been too brusque in his questions; he'd made Lucy furious and she'd made him furious right back. Terrizi, who had been weaned on the noisy brawls of a big Italian family and the noisier loving reconciliations washed down with tears and Chianti, thought of that battle nostalgically. From the start, Mrs. Ramsdale had always been able to get a rise out of the inspector.

Almost as soon as he poured out the coffee, black and strong, and sat down in the chair opposite McDougal, he began to stress that Lucy was a considerably

* *To Spite Her Face*

92

more reliable witness than his mother. "You know Mama."

The inspector's lips twitched; he knew Lucy too. And he knew he was in no shape for a confrontation. "Go and talk to her yourself. She's always up by now, and she said her guest would sleep till noon."

This wasn't at all what Sergeant Terrizi had in mind. "You'd get more out of what she says. I mean, you could sift through and know when she's telling it straight and when she's thinking in loops."

"I'm not on the case," McDougal said, in a flat voice. "If there *is* a case, which hasn't been established. The man has a bad heart—he dies of a heart attack. An easy way out. I envy him."

As soon as he'd said it, part of his mind despised the cheap bathos of it. But the other part stayed in a wallow of bitter self-pity. He took a sip of coffee without tasting it. He hadn't eaten for eighteen hours, and he didn't care if he never ate again. He had been dreading the possibility that Lucy might arrive with a breakfast tray, one of her kippered-herring-and-hot-applebread deals. But when Lucy appeared now at the open door of the studio, he found himself dully resentful that she wasn't carrying a thing. He felt cheated of the chance to refuse all sustenance. Lucy was wearing her most becoming gardening outfit—blue denim jacket and pants and a wide brimmed yellow straw hat—and she seemed annoyingly cheerful and unconcerned.

"Good morning. I'm just on my way to fertilize the iris."

She always got fertilizer too close to the plants. Well, let her. He barely nodded in acknowledgment of her "good morning."

It was Sergeant Terrizi who leaped up and urged her to come in. He almost threw himself across the

93

room to unlatch the screen door before McDougal could say something negative like "get lost." The sergeant couldn't imagine anyone ever saying "get lost" to Lucy Ramsdale, but then, he could never have imagined seeing the inspector drunk, especially at 7 A.M. It was a morning for the unimaginable to come true.

"I was just telling the inspector we'd have to consult you, Mrs. Ramsdale. He wanted me to talk to you myself, but I figured three heads are better than two."

"That sounds like the old 'Two can live as cheaply as one.' Except nobody ever says that any more. Even one can't live as cheaply as one now." She was rattling on while she sized up McDougal's condition. "Nicky, will you get another cup?" She took off her sun hat and fluffed her curly white hair. "And bring the bottle of brandy. We need a slug in our coffee."

The sergeant's eyes, shiny as black olives, shone even more as he watched the size of the slug she put into McDougal's cup. Why hadn't he thought of that himself? But coming from him, it would have seemed disrespectful. Coming from Lucy, it was a hair of the dog among friends.

McDougal took a sip, then a deep swallow, and this time he actually tasted. He began to feel the first stirrings of warmth through his iron-cold despair. He said, being careful to articulate, "I am not going to be involved in this case."

So there *was* a case. Lucy felt such a leap of thankfulness she wanted to gallop full speed; instead, she pulled hard on the reins. "I don't blame you a bit," she said coolly. "Let them get Hanson down from Hartford. After all, you're retired, and as long as he has your old job he should do the dirty work."

Sergeant Terrizi looked at her reproachfully; some ally.

McDougal smoldered. Inspector Hanson, the head of the Connecticut State Police, homicide division, was good, but he, McDougal, was better. Two years ago, it had been Hanson, then chief of detectives, who had had to tell him, reluctantly, after half of Hartford already knew, that his wife was having an affair. And when Hanson learned what had happened with Eileen now . . .

"There may be no case anyway," he said sullenly. "The man probably died of a heart attack."

"Good," Lucy said, although her own heart was plummeting down a deep well of disappointment. "A really tricky murder takes too much work to solve."

The sergeant was so indignant at this treachery he had a professional lapse; he blurted out, "Mama isn't the only one who says Dilman was poisoned."

"Larry Dilman's dead? My God!" She was jolted out of her new role of playing it cool. "If he was murdered, I know who did it."

McDougal made a sour face. "You always know who did it. And you're always wrong."

"Just try to prove I'm wrong this time. Georgina Hampter's the only one who had a real motive. Larry was pressuring her terribly." She repeated the scraps of conversation she'd overheard between Larry and Georgina.

Terrizi was relieved to have this solid backing for his mother's suspicions. "The inspector was saying not ten minutes ago that Dilman must have had something on her."

McDougal sat up a bit straighter. Had he said that? Yes, he must have. He took a gulp of coffee and listened.

"I mean, to make the Hampter dame eat crow like that."

"But not to make her kill Dilman," McDougal said.

"Not the kind of reactionary she is. It's not consistent."

"You don't know her as well as I do." Lucy's temper was crackling like heat lightning. "That woman would do anything—absolutely anything. Anybody who'd lug a fetus in a jar all over town—don't talk to me about consistency."

"I wouldn't dream of talking to *you* about consistency."

"The Frankenstein of little minds," Lucy said, with contempt. "The police are consistent and look what happens. They let a computer muck up traffic—and people like Georgina will get away with murder because the machine punched the wrong card."

"You have no proof whatsoever against Mrs. Hampter. You don't even know it was murder. You're leaping to conclusions."

"Where else would I leap?" Lucy asked reasonably. "A conclusion is what we want."

"Condemning an innocent person is a conclusion?"

"Who's talking about an innocent person? All I want you to do is arrest Georgina."

The sergeant was warmed by this clash, so like old times, and decided it was time to bring up his big gun in support of McDougal. "I called the police doctor right after Dilman died and told him the—uh—setup." Terrizi delicately forebore repeating the conversation in clinical detail. "He says if it was poison, judging from the symptoms it had to start working pretty fast—say, ten or fifteen minutes at the most. Everybody says Dilman was OK till he ate, and Georgina Hampter's the only one who wasn't around then."

"It can't have been food, because we all ate exactly the same thing: that damn shish kebab. Actually, it wasn't bad, but all the fuming and fussing; it went on

96

for hours. They built up that fire enough to roast an ox and then the librarian and her—"

She started to say "beau" and hesitated. The last time she'd used the word, a fellow volunteer at the Thrift Shop had remarked that "beau" was so dated it sounded Victorian. That had stung. But Lucy loathed "boy friend." She compromised.

"—her friend, Jeff Whosis. Larry invited Marcy Coving—that's the librarian—to stay for dinner so Jeff stayed too, and that meant whittling more sticks . . . and Jeff got so annoyed at Larry he nearly ran him through."

Terrizi was looking too interested.

"Larry was *not* stabbed," Lucy said. "If he was poisoned—as of course he was—then Georgina Hampter either picked a poison that doesn't work right away or she sneaked back later and dropped something into his drink."

Lucy went on building the case against Georgina, but the inspector was no longer listening. Something Lucy had said earlier had nearly pierced through his fog, but the trouble was, he couldn't remember what. Whatever it was, he connected it, in a slippery way, with the *New York Times* garden page. His mind floundered and twisted, in the effort to reach something he knew was important. Cornell . . . professor at Cornell. . . .

A shaft of sun struck him in the eyes, and he blinked and ducked his head, suddenly aware of being unshaved and unkempt. The old deep-rooted instinct for orderliness stirred—get out a razor and toothbrush . . . shower . . . cold shower—but he sat inert.

Lucy, who had been watching him, got up and said matter-of-factly, "If you want to take a shower before I get back, you'll have time. I'll collect a few things at the house and scramble the eggs over here."

McDougal mumbled something about "not hungry."

"I'm not thinking of you. But Sergeant Terrizi is starved." Usually she said "Nicky," but she wanted to sound official. "He's been up all night, and he's the one who'll have to work on this case. And I won't have him hearing the results of the autopsy on an empty stomach."

Sergeant Terrizi looked confused but grateful.

On her way out, Lucy passed the closed door of the studio's bedroom, and as clearly as if she could see through walls, she knew there was a bottle of Scotch on the bedside table. Probably about empty by now. He's been at it all night. If we can get him back into his routine, he won't be so apt to go on drinking this morning. He'd feel messy.

She longed to know what had happened with the ex-wife; it took almost saintly patience not to ask. "Let's say twenty minutes. OK?"

The inspector didn't eat the scrambled eggs with Smithfield ham, but he did down a piece of dry toast and three more cups of black coffee, this time without brandy. He still looked caved in, somehow, but his eyes were no longer glazed; they were merely sunken. He had showered and shaved, and he was wearing good gray slacks and a white shirt instead of his around-the-yard khaki fatigues. Lucy, who was ready to seize on straws in the wind and twist them to any desired shape, took McDougal's choice of clothes as a good sign. If the autopsy turned out the way she expected, he could put on a jacket and go right out to investigate. She sensed during breakfast that he was already trying to think something out; she recognized a special abstracted air that had nothing to do with personal emotional problems. Nicky sensed it too. Both of them kept quiet and ate their eggs, but occasionally they exchanged a conspiratorial look.

It was easier for the sergeant to keep quiet: for one thing, he went on eating much longer; for another, he was used to deferring to the inspector. Lucy, who never deferred even to God, began to get restive. Why didn't they phone and find out if there was anything in on the autopsy?

For the first time, she took in that Larry Dilman, whom she'd known for over thirty years, was being cut up to find out how he'd died. She tried to feel horrified, or at least grieved, but she couldn't manage it. Alive, Larry had hurt too many people. And if his death could be unnatural enough—and interesting enough—to be occupational therapy for McDougal, then that seemed only just.

Lucy thought with something like pleasure of the exciting news she might be able to tell Alison when her guest finally woke up: "Larry Dilman was *murdered*." Alison would positively gloat. As she pictured the scene, she finally did feel a tweak of conscience, or perhaps more a need to distinguish her own feelings from Alison's vindictive glee. I'm not *glad* he's dead. After all, he never did anything to me. But even Barbara will be better off with him dead. He was hell bent on getting rid of her. It would be just like him not to have made a will. But a widow's legally entitled to a third of the estate. Or is it a half? A half sounded more nicely rounded. Lucy decided generously that Barbara could remarry—and soon. She wouldn't go so far as to furnish a candidate, but she would give her approval and send a decent wedding present. Did Connecticut laws provide a share of the estate for the daughter too? If not, something would have to be done about poor Joan. Lucy made a mental note to ask her own lawyer about that. Douglas Brill certainly wouldn't mourn Larry's death. Neither would young Jeff Whosis. His Marcy would be shocked and shaken, but that wouldn't last long. It had been Lawrence Dilman, the famous author of *Wayward the World*, rather than Larry Dilman, the crepy-necked Don Juan, whom Marcy had been drawn to. And of course the girl had been even more impressed when Larry made Georgina back down. What was it Larry had said in the greenhouse about not wanting Marcy to know how he'd managed that? She could see his eyebrows peaking up mischievously: "Someday I may tell you how I did it."

With sudden cold clarity, Lucy thought, But now he can't tell me, ever, and he didn't get Georgina to put anything on paper. Georgina promised she'd make a statement next week. And now Larry's dead.

"That's why she had to kill him right away," Lucy said aloud.

Sergeant Terrizi, who had been about to spear his fourth slice of Smithfield ham, put down his fork. "If you mean Mrs. Hampter, like I said before, she's the only one who didn't have a chance to poison him near enough to dinnertime."

"She could have," McDougal said, "with a skewer."

Lucy and Sergeant Terrizi looked at each other with leaping alarm. The inspector was in even worse shape than they'd thought.

"Shish kebab," McDougal said. "On the garden page of the *New York Times*. A Cornell professor."

"Mac," Lucy said gently, "why don't you take a sleeping pill and lie down for a while?"

"Bellyache and convulsions," McDougal said, more to himself. "And vomiting. A poison, all right. But it acts as a violent heart stimulant."

"What does, sir?"

"Oleander. The skewer."

"But the skewers were cut from a maple. And oleander doesn't grow around here. Only down south and on the West Coast."

Lucy banged her fist down so hard that the coffee cups clattered. "Like hell it doesn't! There's a huge oleander in that greenhouse. I saw it myself."

Suddenly her face crumpled, and she blinked back tears. "I thought Mac had lost his mind and would have to be locked up." Her smile came like a rainbow as she looked at him. "And all the time you were only being brilliant."

The inspector had never seen Lucy cry, and instead of making him edgy, it had the odd effect of sharpening his mental faculties. He seemed to be thinking more clearly. Too clearly.

"I'm so brilliant," he said ruefully, "that I forgot one shish kebab looks like another. How would the murderer know which was which?"

"Mama would know. She was serving. But if Mama wanted to kill somebody, she wouldn't use poison. Too slow."

"Tomato!" Lucy said in almost a screech. Both men stared at her. "I mean—the one without. Barbara told your mother not to put any tomato on Larry's."

"Phone your mother and ask her if anybody else could have heard that."

The sergeant started for the phone extension in the bedroom.

McDougal said hurriedly, "Use the one out here. We may think of more questions while you're talking to her."

Terrizi dialed. "Mama—" There was a torrent of sound from the other end.

"Mama, I was not helling around with strange women. I had to stay at the hospital till Mr. Dilman died.... Yeah, we think so too.... Mama, listen, when his wife told you not to put tomato on his shish kebab. ... *Listen,* Mama; I know you didn't forget.... No, Mrs. Dilman did *not* say a tomato killed him. But when she told you *no* tomato on his skewer, could anybody else have heard?"

He put a hand over the receiver. "Mama says anybody who wasn't stone deaf would have heard. She says Mrs. Dilman told her the same thing four or five times—in the kitchen, on the terrace...."

"Ask her if she put all the scraps from the meal in the outside garbage can?"

Terrizi transmitted this question. "You *what?*" In a dazed voice he said, "Mr. Dilman left so much good meat you brought it home and gave it to the dog next door? Holy Jesus, Mama.... No. I'm not blaspheming. I'm praying. We think the meat may have been poisoned. Listen, Mama, are you sure it was from Mr. Dilman's plate?"

He turned from the phone again. "She knows it was Dilman's because he was the only one who left any food on his plate. She put the meat on the Rossettis' back porch last night, in the dog's bowl, and she knows he's still alive because he's peeing on her rosebush right now."

McDougal looked so dejected at this refutation, however unscientific, of his theory that Lucy said,

"Nicky, ask your mother to go next door and check the dog's dish. The dog may not have eaten it yet."

The inspector said urgently, wishfully, "Have her grab the meat and we'll get a lab analysis this morning."

Terrizi said into the phone, "Mama. This is important. Run get that bowl this minute. The stuff could kill the dog. Then come tell me. I'll hang on."

They were all hanging on, too tense to talk, while they waited.

Suddenly the phone crackled to life again. The sergeant listened and said in a funereal voice, "Yes, Mama. . . . And Mrs. Rossetti didn't throw it out, so the dog must have eaten it. . . . Mama, I don't know when I'll be home. I shaved in the car."

In the outpouring of sound, Lucy distinctly heard Mrs. Terrizi say, "What gives with the inspector?"

Terrizi hunched his broad shoulders. "Not now, Mama. I'm very busy. *I'm at the inspector's.* . . . Yes, Mama, Mrs. Ramsdale fed us. . . . No, she wasn't poisoned last night. Nobody said it was your cooking. . . ." And, on a rising note of despair, "Mama, I gotta go. Good-bye."

When he hung up, the palms of his hands were wet. He took out his handkerchief and wiped off the receiver carefully.

"Looks like the poison wasn't in the shish kebab, so that lets out Mrs. Hampter."

"It was probably a plain heart attack, anyway," the inspector said.

"You weren't there and I was." Lucy was furious. "The whole thing was like one of those irritating murder mysteries when the rich bastard invites a lot of people who hate him to come for the weekend and talks about changing his will—or threatens somebody with exposure if they don't do so-and-so."

"What could he expose about Georgina Hampter? Everybody in Wingate knows she's a ranting fanatic."

" 'Pillaress of rectitude,' " Lucy said thoughtfully. "He was being sarcastic. So he knew her when she wasn't erect."

The phone rang and Terrizi lifted it automatically. "This may be Chief Salter. I told him I'd be here. . . . Mama! I told you I'm very busy. . . . No, I don't need to hear about the other dogs in the neighborhood. . . . Dead! The Spolipskys' dog's dead? . . . The vet says she was fed poisoned meat? . . . No, Mama, I didn't mean to sound tickled to death. . . . Of course I'm sorry for Mrs. Spolipsky." Over his shoulder, he muttered to his companions, "Mean bitch—always grabbing any food around. Bit the United Parcel man in the ass. . . . Yes, Mama, I'm listening. . . . Mrs. Spolipsky thinks it was a burglar who wanted to get rid of the dog? Mama, you just let her think that."

# 10

The greenhouse glistened in the midmorning sun, but inside the air had the cool, earthy freshness of newly watered plants. Sergeant Terrizi had worked in a Wingate greenhouse all during his teens, after school and on Saturdays, and he was as much at home here as a child in its mother's womb. He had never read Roethke's poems on a nurseryman—he wasn't a man for poetry—but he shared the same feelings: "In my veins, in my bones I feel it—the small waters seeping upward."

Walking down the center aisle between plants, his senses responded as a gardener's instead of a cop's. He looked with love at some tiny mauve orchids, "delicate as a young bird's tongue," and noted, with approval, the healthy leaves of the Alpha geraniums. They'd be ready to set out right after Memorial Day. Automatically, he pinched off one yellowed leaf.

It wasn't until he heard Inspector McDougal come in, perhaps a minute later, that the cop in Terrizi shook free of the spell. "Haven't spotted it yet," he said, in that too-brisk tone one uses to make up for a lapse in efficiency. "If I could have another look at that sketch Mrs. Ramsdale did for us. . . ."

McDougal took out the small scratch pad Lucy had sketched on, tore off the top sheet, and handed it over. He didn't need to glance at it again; the sketch was imprinted line for line behind his eyeballs. Like a tightrope walker, he had to focus on just one thing to keep from falling. He had told Chief Salter of the Wingate police, "If my theory is right, I'll handle the case for you. If not . . ." He had left the rest hanging up in the air, as his own life seemed to be hanging—over a void. His eyes were already searching, left, right, down the length of the greenhouse to where a bamboo curtain stretched from one side to the other, and from ceiling to floor. No oleander. He walked up and down, his long legs striding like stilts, while he examined each plant close to. No oleander. Disappointment was so bitter it came out harshly in his voice. "Lucy was wrong."

"She said she was sitting in a wicker chair with a high back, and the plant was right across from her. So where's the chair?" The sergeant snapped his fingers. "Whadda ya bet—?" He trotted to the bamboo curtain and yanked at the side cord. The curtain creaked protestingly, went up a few feet, and stopped. Terrizi tugged again, then gave up and dove underneath.

"It's here!" he shouted. "This is it. Just like she said."

McDougal held up the bamboo curtain enough to duck under it, and then unfolded to his height of six feet three. The oleander came just to his chin. Terrizi was already circling around to the back of the plant, which was set against the right-hand wall. "Branch hacked off here," he said; he almost sang it.

McDougal stooped to examine the raw whitish spot where a branch had been slashed off with no attempt at concealing the damage. "Ought to be a knife around. She would have had to whittle the skewer in here." The *she* was either a Freudian slip or, more likely, a subconscious expression of gratitude to Lucy, who wanted a "she" as a murderer.

The sergeant remembered a wooden rack of knives attached to a post near the front door of the greenhouse. He raced back to examine it; one slot in the knife rack was empty. "But the gardener may have taken it out this morning. He used the sprinklers early in here. That's why he lowered the bamboo curtain, so's he wouldn't wet the chairs. This is Saturday. He's probably off for most of the day, but he'd have to come back to lock up."

The inspector had gone over to the wicker chair with the high back and was staring at the seat cushion; the chintz was patterned after the most famous sunflower of all, and he thought Lucy must have felt as if she were sitting on a fake Van Gogh. Terrizi watched him lift the cushion—portentous moment—and they gazed down together at the find: one dead June bug, squashed.

"Mark that Exhibit B," McDougal said. "Whoever sat there after Lucy left was heavy enough to squash a large hard-shelled bug, my dear Watson."

Terrizi grinned; he was so happy that the sun pouring in seemed a part of his radiant contentment. They had not only found an oleander, but a recently hacked oleander, just as McDougal had predicted. And, much more important, the inspector was sounding almost jaunty.

"Call the state barracks and ask them to send a

man over to pick up these other knives and have them tested, just in case," McDougal said. "Phone over there."

While Terrizi was phoning—"Yeah, traces of oleander. . . . O-L-E-A-N-D-E-R, it's a poisonous plant that may have been used as a skewer. . . . No, not like a South American dart, wise guy"—the inspector opened the side door into the passageway and estimated the length of time it would take to cover the distance—approximately fifteen feet—to the kitchen. At a run, or even a fast walk, say, twenty seconds. Allow five minutes to sharpen the skewer, plus the twenty seconds in the passageway; two minutes to remove the no-tomato shish kebab from the original skewer and rethread it onto the substitute. . . . Probably under eight minutes altogether. Mrs. Terrizi had been dashing all over the place: the living room, the terrace, the garage for more briquets. They could pin down the times she'd been out of the kitchen, if they could pin down Mrs. Terrizi. Thinking of Mrs. Terrizi's volatile nature, the inspector thought, It's like those old recipes for jugged hare: "First catch a plump hare and skin it."

He had felt like skinning Mrs. Terrizi an hour before, when they'd stopped by to ask what she'd done with the skewers after dinner. She had put them in the incinerator along with the other garbage. "Who saves wooden sticks?" she had asked reasonably. "You expect me to put 'em away with the silver?"

Terrizi was saying on the phone, ". . . and tell them to dust for fingerprints before they send the knives to the lab."

McDougal guessed the distance from the oleander to the knife rack to be almost forty feet. It would have taken time—maybe thirty seconds more—for the murderer to replace the knife in the rack. And he certainly wouldn't have spared time to clean it right then. (By now, the inspector was thinking of the murderer, from habit, as "he.") Too risky to carry the knife around and get rid of it later. So the chances were he might have hidden it in the nearest place.

McDougal went back and fiddled with the cord on the bamboo curtain till he got it to roll up properly. (Anything out of order was a hostile force that had to be conquered.) He poked in the earth around the oleander, and then in all the other plant tubs: no knife, not even wood shavings. He went to the high-backed chair again and prodded the uptilted cushion to make sure nothing had been slipped inside. He was about to put it down on the seat again when he spotted something else: a piece of wood splinter several inches long, on the floor just inside the front leg of the chair. He got down on his knees, wrapped his handkerchief around his right hand, and tried to scoop up the splinter, but this was like trying to pick up a needle while wearing boxing gloves. Instead of poking the splinter out where he could get at it, he managed to knock it much farther underneath. The sides of the chair extended so low that McDougal, even on his knees, could no longer see his quarry. He stretched out flat on the floor, so that he could get his head underneath, and managed to paw the wood fragment back out within reaching distance. Sun was sifting down through the rolled-over arm of the chair, casting a filigree pattern of wicker on the tile floor. And the shadow of something else caught in the wicker—a longish, thin object.

Sergeant Terrizi replaced the receiver of the wall phone and turned to see the inspector prostrate, long legs protruding. He heard McDougal's muffled voice saying what sounded like "shot in the arm."

Who—where—how? Terrizi drew his gun and whirled around, but saw nobody.

"I think . . . got . . . knife in arm," McDougal mumbled.

He'd been stabbed! Terrizi raced back and knelt beside the prostrate inspector. "Lie still. I'll slit your sleeve and see how bad." He laid down his gun, took out his pocket knife, which had four keen blades and a bottle opener, and was trying to find which sleeve to slash when he heard a peculiar snorting noise; the inspector was laughing.

"Not me, the chair arm," McDougal said, rolling over. "I think the knife's hidden in there. See—the shadow looks the right shape. I spotted the splinter."

Terrizi felt silly but relieved.

The opening in the rolled-over arm was underneath where the arm joined the side, a gap of perhaps a half inch, too narrow to get his hand into. The inspector turned the chair upside down. "Have to cut it. I'll hold it while you cut."

The sergeant hesitated. He couldn't see why the knife was all that important; nobody these days would be stupid enough to leave fingerprints. But he sensed that McDougal needed some tangible thing to hold onto as evidence, something larger than a splinter of wood that might or might not be oleander. He said mildly, "It'll sure mess up the chair."

"We'll buy them a new one," the inspector said recklessly.

That settled it. Terrizi attacked with the largest blade on his pocket knife, and McDougal held the chair as steady as he could while the sergeant sawed and hacked.

"Sergeant! Have you gone mad? What are you doing?"

Terrizi whirled around, knife in hand, to see Lawrence Dilman's widow standing in the side doorway.

"I'm sorry if we startled you, Mrs. Dilman."

"The sergeant was acting on my instructions," McDougal said. "I'm the one who should apologize." He introduced himself. "Chief Salter has asked us to make an investigation and we got a search warrant, but we were anxious not to disturb you too early, after all you've been through."

"I still don't understand what you're doing." Barbara Dilman now sounded as sensibly controlled as she looked. She was wearing a tailored navy blue robe, her short hair was neatly brushed, and her face was as self-contained as an egg.

"Perhaps you'd better sit down." McDougal indicated a chair that hadn't been knifed. Barbara Dilman, walking past the upside-down chair, managed to convey in silence what she thought of *that*.

She was one of those women who sits down and seems instantly, precisely arranged. "I'll tell you what happened. It was that librarian." Her voice, no longer quite so controlled, was quiet but venomous. "That girl invited herself here with a trumped-up excuse and made an out-and-out play for my husband. So he had to prove he wasn't old and sick. He kicked up his heels and drank too much and raced around. He even climbed those steep stairs to his old office over the garage. His heart couldn't take it—and that girl is responsible for his death."

Sergeant Terrizi had formed a respectful but fondly admiring impression of Marcy Coving at the hospital the night before. She had brought in coffee and sandwiches, she hadn't once yapped hysterically, and she had managed to quiet Dilman's daughter while the wife was in with the patient. He said, "But if your husband didn't die of a heart attack—"

"Of course it was a heart attack. I was a cardio-vascular technician. I know."

The inspector said, "But you didn't think so at first. You waited to call an ambulance."

"Because it started out as stomach pains and nausea. But then later the symptoms changed. He—" For the first time, she faltered.

"You mustn't try to give us details right now. I know how painful it must be for you. But you're certainly entitled to an explanation of this—uh—destroying of property. We were looking for a crucial piece of evidence. We think your husband may have been poisoned."

The inspector had to admire the way she took it: almost clinically. "The vomiting," she said. "And he didn't respond when I gave him oxygen. And finally the convulsions." The technician's impersonal tone changed; she sounded bewildered and sad. "I'd been so cross at him for the way he'd acted all evening. And he'd been so sarcastic to me. Suddenly it was as if I couldn't do anything right. I resented his blaming the shish kebab; I knew it couldn't be that. Even Lucy Ramsdale told me how good it was."

So good it killed the Spolipskys' dog, Sergeant Terrizi thought.

"I only left him alone in the bedroom for five or ten minutes. Joan came to the door and said Mrs. Ramsdale's car was here, so I went out to the driveway and said good-bye to them. By the time I got back, Larry was much worse. That's when I called the ambulance and gave him oxygen. But he *did* have a heart

112

attack, right after we got to the hospital. The doctor will tell you. He's a very fine heart man . . . he didn't say anything about poison."

"He didn't want to worry you," the sergeant said. And he may have thought you poisoned your husband. When a man dies, *cherchez la* wife.

"Something put in his wine," Barbara Dilman said. "It must have been done that way, because he seemed fine before dinner. That girl was the only one sitting with him; she didn't want me there."

Lucy Ramsdale had said, "Larry insisted that Marcy Coving eat with him. And he was so unpleasant to his wife—he practically told her to scram—that Doug and I had to ask her to join us."

Terrizi looked expectantly at the inspector, waiting to hear how he'd counter this twisted account from the widow, and saw with dismay that McDougal's face was now somber, withdrawn; he was staring over Mrs. Dilman's head, not seeing her.

"Inspector," he said loudly, "I think we could tell Mrs. Dilman the poison was not in the wine."

McDougal looked at him blankly.

Terrizi hung on. "You said you wanted to ask Mrs. Dilman about the skewers. For the shish kebab. I mean, what kind."

The inspector, recalled from his private brooding, frowned. Terrizi was taking too much on himself. This wasn't the moment to ask about the skewers. Too leading a question.

"The skewers?" Barbara Dilman looked puzzled. "They were natural wood. We soaked them before they were used."

Terrizi said, "Were they soaking in the kitchen when Georgina Hampter was here?"

"The last two, yes. Mrs. Terrizi had them in one of the sinks." Her hands clenched. "If Larry hadn't asked that girl to stay for dinner . . . the man she was with cut off more branches of—"

"The oleander?" Terrizi cut in swiftly before the inspector could stop him.

"Good lord, no! When I was working in Florida, we had a case brought into emergency that looked like a coronary—cardioactive glucosides—like an overdose of heart stimulants, when—" Her eyes widened. "Is that —is that how you think Larry was poisoned?"

"It's only a guess, so far. But somebody has cut this oleander recently." McDougal indicated the bush.

"Is that the oleander? I'm afraid I'm stupid about plants. Larry's last wife built the greenhouse, and the gardener's the only one now who knows all the names. He prunes bushes so constantly Larry complained they were manicured. He may have done that himself."

"It's not manicured, it's hacked," Terrizi said.

"And so is that perfectly good chair," she said, with spirit. "I still don't understand why you should hack it up."

"If you'd like us to demonstrate," McDougal said suddenly. Dilman's wife with her air of innocence—*Is that the oleander? I'm afraid I'm stupid about plants*— had infuriated him out of all proportion. No woman was going to dupe him again. This one had been startled into admitting she knew about oleander—probably knew we'd check her job record—and then she'd tried to backtrack. So give her a push. "Sergeant, let's finish this job, since Mrs. Dilman is so curious about what we could possibly be looking for. Perhaps we'll be able to show her."

Terrizi didn't like the inspector's tone. Too savagely sarcastic—mean—as if he were accusing the widow straight out: We'll confront you with the evidence and you'll sing a different tune. Sort of third-degree stuff. As a feeble gesture of apology, he said, "We'll see the chair gets mended, ma'am." And if we don't find a knife, he added silently, you can sue us for damages.

But the knife was there, a pruning knife with a dark wood handle. The inspector used his handkerchief again, this time more effectively. As soon as he'd withdrawn the knife, he thrust it almost under the widow's nose. "We'll have it tested for traces of oleander."

She shrank back. "But—but who else besides me would know that oleander's a poison?"

For some reason, the question—or perhaps her authentic-sounding terror—jolted McDougal back to something like normal. "That's what we have to find out," he said. "Maybe somebody trying to frame you. If it would make you more comfortable to call a lawyer, of course that's your right."

"I have to call Larry's lawyer anyway. I already called his publisher and his literary agent this morning, but the publisher had gone to the country for the weekend, and it took me so long to reach him I forgot about the lawyer. He's an old friend of Larry's."

"Do you happen to know if your husband made a will?"

"I'm sure he did. Because I asked him to right after we were married."

"I would strongly suggest you talk to your lawyer before you say anything more."

"But I have nothing to hide. And I'm not the least ashamed of what I did. I'd worked in hospitals for fifteen years and I'd seen patients fall in love with a nurse or a therapist or somebody, but a lot of those marriages cracked up. I have a friend who gave up her nursing career, and then her husband died without changing his will and she had to go to court. . . . Anyway, I wanted to keep my job at the hospital—I loved it—but Larry wouldn't let me. He wanted me to spend all my time looking after *him*. So I thought it was only fair that he make some arrangement about my future."

And then did you arrange his future? McDougal thought. With your nest nicely feathered, you could afford to. You might have preferred being a widow to being a divorcee. More dignified. He tried to focus on what she was saying, but instead he heard his ex-wife's voice so clearly that Barbara Dilman's faded and blurred before it finally came through again.

"And I asked him to set up a trust fund for Joan because if she got a lump sum all at once she'd turn it over to a hippie commune or something. She's simply not capable of handling her own finances."

"And you're not capable of handling me!" Joan said. She had come into the greenhouse through the same door as her stepmother. The quivering intensity Lucy had noticed the day before was even more pronounced, and the deep-socketed eyes were feverishly bright as she looked at Terrizi. "Sergeant, I listened on the extension upstairs when you were talking to somebody about a poisoned skewer. And I wanted to tell you that Barbara is the one who insisted on having shish kebab. Larry wanted tournedos; he l-loved tournedos. But she wouldn't let him have them."

"It was simply a matter of cholesterol," Barbara Dilman said. "Too much beef was bad for him."

"And now his cholesterol's zero." Joan laughed hysterically, on and on, till Barbara slapped her.

When the girl had quieted down to hiccups, Barbara said to McDougal, "I'll give her a tranquilizer."

"The kind you gave Larry?" Joan said.

# 11

Lucy Ramsdale was as restless as a volcano that wants to erupt and can't because some malevolent Fate has clamped the lid on.

Four different friends had called to ask if she'd heard Larry Dilman had died of a heart attack early that morning. Each time she had managed to restrain herself because she'd promised McDougal not to drop even a hint of an investigation, but the wear and tear on her ego was fierce. It had given her some minor satisfaction to be able to say she had been at the Dilmans' the night before for dinner and that Larry had complained of a stomachache and retired early. Following the ritual pattern among the over-sixty set for such occasions, she described how gay Larry had been earlier in the evening. "I hadn't seen him in such high spirits in years." All her listeners were of an age to savor that touch; it made them feel hopeful that when death came within hailing distance they too would be caught laughing. Lucy carefully didn't say why Larry was so exuberant; she was candid by nature but not mean, and she had no intention of throwing Barbara Dilman and Marcy Coving to the mercy of ravening tongues. If she let slip so much as one meaty morsel, the Wingate grapevine, which grew faster than kudzu, would have carried the word all over town by mid-morning that Larry had got drunk and made a fool of himself over the high school librarian and that the overexcitement had killed him.

None of the callers mentioned book banning; sudden death was so much more titillating to talk about. For Lucy, it would have been much more titillating if she could have spilled all she knew. The one friend she could have a really juicy postmortem with was Alison Moffat. But Alison had accepted the weekend invitation with the firm proviso that Lucy would let her sleep. "I do not share your girlish joy in the new day dawning. I'm cradled in the arms of insomnia until three or four A.M., and *then* I sleep like a baby. If you wake me, I'll kill you with my own bare tongue."

Lucy held off for a while, partly because every time the phone rang she hoped it would be the inspector or Sergeant Terrizi with fresh news. They had had the preliminary autopsy report before they went off, and it looked like poison, all right. But she was exasperated that they hadn't called her instantly, as soon as they'd checked on the greenhouse. After all, who was it who'd remembered that Larry's shish kebab could be spotted as No tomato? Where credit was due, Lucy wanted every last ounce of it. As she got madder and madder, she even thought, I could have rented my studio to Doug Brill last night and then where would Mac be? Out in the cold. Back in some dreary little motel room. It's high time he showed a little gratitude for all I've done.

Once, in an argument with her husband, Hal had accused her of being inconsistent, and Lucy had said, "Inconsistency is one of my chief charms."

Five minutes after fuming about the inspector's ingratitude, she was peering into the freezer trying to decide what might tempt him for dinner. Shrimp fondue was one of his favorites, but she had a feeling that people who were in a serious state of emotional depression shouldn't eat shrimp. There was no scientific evidence to support this, but Lucy didn't need scientific evidence, any more than a witch needs it to know which newt to omit from the stew. She debated whether beef-and-kidney pie mightn't be the best choice. A good shell steak would be even better, but she didn't have any in the freezer, and the idea of leaving the telephone, which might blare with real news at any minute, to drive into the village and pick up meat, smacked too much of selflessness. Lucy was a loving, thoughtful friend to people she cared about, but never selfless.

By nine forty-one, the thoughtful hostess had convinced herself that Alison would be furious if she were made to waste time sleeping when there were such fascinating developments to talk about. At nine fifty-three, she was fixing a breakfast tray with her best china, Spode Wickerdell, and had broken off one dogwood blossom in lieu of a rose for the bud vase. It wasn't that Alison would notice these special touches, but they pleased the giver. She had made fresh coffee and was considering Eggs Benedict when she was surprised to see Alison billowing into the kitchen. Her guest was wearing the same costume she'd worn out to dinner the night before, but without the piled-up hairdo.

"Darling, what blessed quiet here," she said in her inimitable voice. "Only ten trucks an hour all night, on that sweet, winding country road."

The road was an interstate, and there *were* rather

a lot of trucks at night, but no other guest had been rude enough to mention it.

"At least you weren't suffocated in California smog. How do you want your eggs?"

"Absent. Black coffee and orange juice. And if you have an English muffin—"

Lucy held off on the big news till she had toasted an English muffin and carried the tray into the living room; Alison was still holding forth.

"Seriously, darling, I haven't had such a good night in years." Alison stretched out her arms, embracing all clean country living. "Remember that play of George Kelly's? Some character who had a frightful hangover was asked how he felt and he said, 'I feel like a glass of warm fish.' That's how Larry must feel this morning. Have you called his wife to ask how his tummyache is?"

"He's dead." Lucy hadn't meant to be so abrupt, but she was annoyed.

"You should never make jokes before the sun is over the yardarm." Alison picked up her glass of orange juice.

"I'm not joking." Lucy tried not to sound gloating. "They called the ambulance right after we left and rushed him to the hospital. He died around four A.M."

Alison went on tilting the glass of juice while the contents dribbled down her front. "What—what did he die of?" Her voice was choked with emotion; her magnificent eyes were dilated with horror, shock, sorrow —the gamut.

Actors! Lucy thought. She doesn't have to be so damn melodramatic. Tragic lost love, indeed. She's hardly seen the man in thirty years. Even when Hal died, I didn't carry on like that.

Lucy was so indignant she abandoned any semblance of caution. "At first they thought it was heart, but now we're quite sure it was poison."

Surprisingly, Alison now radiated cheerful interest. In a normal, gossipy tone, she said, "You mean Barbara slipped something into his drink?"

"Not his drink. It looks as if it was done with the shish kebab. A substitute skewer of oleander." Not having had any phone call to confirm this, the statement was wishful but delivered with authority. She saw with irritation that Alison had shifted back to her stricken tragedienne role, with gestures: hands clutching face.

"A skewer couldn't poison anybody. That's impossible."

"When Jeff Whosis sharpened the original skewers—" She meant to go on, he used maple, but Alison cut in sharply.

"Jeff Solent had nothing to do with this. He was with me every minute during that time."

"You don't even know what time it would have been." Lucy came near adding, And stop acting like an hysterical mama. Nobody's accusing your boy. But Alison looked so upset—and this time it didn't seem an act—that Lucy took pity on her. "I never meant Jeff was the murderer."

"Don't even use that horrible word."

Really, Alison was being quite impossible.

"If you'd stop emoting and let me finish. . . . Georgina Hampter's obviously the one. She was in the kitchen earlier and heard Barbara say, 'No tomato on Mr. Dilman's shish kebab.' That's how she knew which one to fix. And we think Larry was blackmailing Georgina some way to make her back down on the books, so she had to remove him."

"She really is an evil woman, isn't she? You'd all be better off if she were out of commission for a while."

"And if she goes to jail she'll never earn time off for good behavior, not that woman."

Alison shifted again. "I think you've made up this whole ridiculous plot because you want to get rid of her."

Lucy bristled. "I'd never put an innocent woman in prison."

"You don't know what you'd do till you've done it." Alison got up and began pacing the floor. "I refuse to go to his funeral. Funerals are barbaric anyhow. When I first went to Hollywood, a director I'd known in the old days on Broadway died, and they buried him in Forest Lawn. They hauled all of us out to that ghastly place in hired limousines, and do you know what the hired chauffeurs wore? Black glasses. Not just dark glasses, *black*. Black for mourning—mourning a man they'd never met. Part of the props for the show. I was so revolted I've never gone to a funeral since. Oh, Lucy, I wish I'd stayed on the Coast. I wish I'd never seen Larry again. They can't ask me to look at him in a coffin."

"Nobody's asking you. I feel the same way. When I die, I want an announcement in all the papers: 'Please Omit Funeral.' If anybody sends flowers for Larry's, they'd damn well better not send oleander."

Alison hunched over and grabbed her stomach as if she were going to retch. "Don't say such things."

Lucy thought, She never really appreciates anybody's good lines but her own. "Come on, now, calm down and drink your coffee. I thought you'd be fascinated by the whole thing, and instead you carry on like Medea."

"What made you say Medea?"

"Would you rather I said Lady Macbeth? I know the inspector would enjoy your doing that hand-wringing turn of Lady Macbeth. He'll be back any minute."

"You mean your inspector? You told me he'd gone for good."

"He's back. He's working on this case." She tried not to sound as satisfied as she felt.

"Then I'm in the way." Alison clapped her hand to what, under the circumstances, could only be called her bosom. "I must leave at once."

"Don't be ridiculous." But ridiculous or not, Lucy couldn't help wishing her guest were emoting somewhere else. McDougal was overwrought enough himself right now, without all this piled on. If Alison goes on this way when he interviews her—but if he waits till Monday she'll be gone. A disheartening postscript occurred to her. "You can't leave Wingate anyway, not till the inspector says so. We're all suspects or something."

Rather to her surprise, Alison didn't explode. She sat huddled in her chair looking like a collapsed dirigible. "I was thinking more of you," she said plaintively. "The last thing you need right now is to have a guest on your hands when you'll be doing your Sherlocking bit." She broke her English muffin in half, as if she were finally going to eat it. But instead she went on breaking each piece into smaller and smaller pieces.

"I *will* be rather busy," Lucy said. "The inspector may want me to take over some of the interviewing. And he likes to talk things over with me."

"Otherwise, he'd never muddle through to whodun-it." Alison's voice rasped with sarcasm.

That tore it. "I really think you'd be happier

alone," Lucy said. "And frankly, you're dreary company right now. I'm sure you could get a room at the Wingate Inn. They have quite a good chef."

"Nobody's cooking could equal yours, darling." Alison playing the penitent. "And I *have* been dreary company this morning. Forgive me for carrying on. Larry isn't worth it. Let's both have some more coffee, and I want to hear all about everything."

# 12

There is nothing in the bylaws or even the unwritten code of the newspaper fraternity that forbids a reporter to have a drink while on duty. The Associated Press man felt he'd earned one anyway; he had interviewed Lawrence Dilman just a few hours before the famous novelist's death. And he had come to get Georgina Hampter's statement that morning, Saturday, instead of waiting till Monday, because with it under his belt he could polish off his story, and a much better story than he'd originally hoped for. The headline already glimmered in his head: AUTHOR FIGHTS BOOK BAN, DIES A WINNER.

He had never met Georgina Hampter before, but he had interviewed at least two dozen of her ilk, and in his view they were kooks in sheep's clothing. Most of the women wore what he thought of as Respectable Frustrated Housewife outfits, and the men, give or take a few stiff-collared pulpit types, might have belonged to Rotary, Kiwanis, Elks, Moose, Lions, or the Merchants' Association of Whatsis.

Georgina Hampter looked richer than most of his female interviewees, although this impression may have been due more to the very large, solid house she lived in. At first glance, she gave off the same impression as the house: large and solidly pillared. When she opened the door, he somehow expected her to say, "Scrape your feet and don't track mud on my carpets."

Instead, she oozed hostess clichés while she led the way through a welter of velvet-upholstered furniture to a corner of the overstuffed living room and settled him in a not-too-uncomfortable chair. "I'm just about to have a midmorning drink. Won't you join me?"

Beer foamed through his mind—it was another very-warm-for-May day—but Mrs. Hampter didn't strike him as the beer-drinking sort, or even the beer-buying sort. Scotch on the rocks? With a layout like this, she ought to run to Chivas Regal.

". . . iced sassafras tea or carrot juice with pineapple."

His ears took in the words numbly and his brain conveyed the message to his nervous system, which shuddered.

"N-nothing, thanks."

He got a brief satisfaction in watching the photographer, who arrived with his gear a few minutes later, fall into the same trap.

"Mr. Ralston says he won't join me in a drink. How about you?"

The photographer, after one incredulous look at his colleague, said, "Sounds fine," but before he could name his choice, he too was offered the specialties of the house. Having committed himself, he was stuck; he chose iced sassafras tea.

His feeling of persecution lightened when the maid brought in the concoctions on a silver tray, not because of the so-called refreshment but because of the maid. She was a tall, beautifully boned young black, with the lovely elongations of a Giacometti sculpture. The photographer could hardly restrain himself from taking shots of her right then and there. On the pretense of trying out camera angles while his colleague was talking to the hostess, he did manage to follow the maid into the hall. "If you want any modeling jobs," he said, "I could give you the name of a good agency in New York."

The girl looked amused. "Thank you, but I tried it and didn't like it. And my fiancé is on the police force here, so I wouldn't want to leave Wingate."

The photographer retreated to the living room; he was so rattled he swallowed half his midmorning drink in one gulp. To take the taste out of his mouth, he seized a small tan cracker and bit; it was like biting into a nutshell, with sound effects.

"Aren't those Japanese rice crackers delicious?" Mrs. Hampter said. "I persuaded the organic foods store here to get in a supply, those and the soybean wafers...."

As she chatted on about soybeans and some kind of hand-ground unbleached flour, the photographer noticed that her rather thick white fingers were clutching her glass too tightly; the glass trembled.

Ralston, the reporter, yanked the conversation back on the track. "Mr. Dilman told me last night you'd agreed to replace all five books in the school library."

"He misunderstood me."

"But several other people heard you. The librarian, for one, told me—"

The gracious-hostess act evaporated. Georgina Hampter's mouth had that sullen look of a rhinocerus's just before the charge. "I'd advise you not to place any credence in what the librarian says. She's a flighty youngster who fell into that job overnight, and she has no moral values whatsoever. She is not a fit person to influence growing minds."

"In what way?"

"We needn't go into that now. I intend to have more to say at our meeting Monday. I do hope you'll come."

Ralston said in a tired voice that he'd expected to wrap up the story on censorship before then. His prized headline, AUTHOR FIGHTS BOOK BAN, DIES A WIN-NER, was growing dimmer and dimmer.

"Of course Mr. Dilman's *Wayward the World* will be replaced at once, out of respect for the dead."

That was something, at least; the reporter made notes.

"And you may quote me as saying his death is a great loss to literature."

She pronounced it *literchoor*. Ralston hoped he could get that into his story. Obviously Lawrence Dilman's death was far from a loss to Georgina Hampter, but he couldn't say that in print: too libelous. Maybe get across the idea by saying Mrs. Hampter seemed to have reneged on her promise after she heard Dilman was dead. Still too strong. "Changed her mind" would be safer. Even with Women's Lib, dames were still allowed to change their minds.

"I'm extremely busy today," Mrs. Hampter said. "So if you need a photograph before you go. . . ."

To get even for the midmorning drink, the photographer shot her at an angle that made her neck look even shorter than it was. This cheered him slightly, and he was even more cheered when his colleague said they'd see the librarian next: "I got her home address."

Chief Salter had gone to inspect a crop of healthy

marijuana which had appeared, inexplicably, growing behind a hedge on the hospital grounds. Inspector McDougal was using the chief's phone in his office at headquarters to check the latest report from the lab on the Dilman autopsy. The medical examiner sounded genial.

"It's *Nerium oleander* all right. Wouldn't have spotted it so soon if you hadn't given us the tip-off. Might even have missed it altogether. Acts a lot like digitalis, and with Dilman having a bum heart, it worked even faster. What put you onto oleander in the first place?"

"Garden page of the Sunday *New York Times*." He explained about the article.

"Probably a big help for Garden Club ladies who want to bump off a husband. Always thought cookouts were kind of a plot against husbands anyway. 'Oh, it's so virile to cook out of doors, dear. And you look so cute in your chef's hat.' We fall for it every time. Dilman came off worse than most of us though. . . ."

McDougal's mind drifted and was instantly pulled to his own troubles as if to a magnet. If Eileen had poisoned him physically, he'd have been better off. But his ex-wife would never have read a garden page; she'd had a standing order with a Hartford florist to deliver fresh bouquets every week, all year round. Maybe if she hadn't had money of her own. . . .

". . . kind of hoping this was a first," the medical examiner said. "But I looked it up in the Gonzalez and Halpern *Toxicology*—"

"So did I." McDougal cut in quickly, to forestall any technical rehash. "But I couldn't be sure till I talked to you. Thanks for getting right onto the autopsy. That clinches it."

"My pleasure. Not often I get an exotic killing. I still say that was brilliant guesswork of yours."

The inspector hung up and tried to feel elated. Instead, he felt as if he were tied to lead weights. His surroundings did nothing to buoy his mood. The walls of the chief's small office were a peeling, dingy, gray-green with fly-specked WANTED posters for decor. The place was so ringed with filing cabinets they looked as if they might advance in formation and overrun the desk and its occupant. Bulging cardboard boxes on top of the cabinets and even on the floor held the over-flow. Citizens of Wingate prided themselves on living in one of the most photogenic towns in Connecticut, and the Town Hall was pillared in the best Colonial tradition; police headquarters, jammed into the base-ment of that building, occupied exactly 1,235 square feet.

McDougal stared at a pile of soggy cardboard coffee containers in the wastebasket beside him and debated whether to order a sandwich and coffee be-fore he went out again. Almost noon now. Lucy had mentioned something about lunch; he ought to call her. But he still hadn't seen Georgina Hampter; that would be the first thing Lucy would ask him about. . . .

At the front desk, the sergeant on duty, Gillian Bayles, was talking to Terrizi. "Mrs. Hampter's done a flip again." He had a slight Jamaican accent that was really more lilt than accent. "Soon as she learned Dil-man was dead, she started heating the witches' bon-fires again. Zora called me after the Associated Press people left and she's foaming at the lips: says she'll give notice. She'd wanted to keep that job till she finished writing her play because it's good money and

131

not much to do. The Hampters always used to go to their place in Florida in the winters, but now Mrs. Hampter keeps hightailing it off to conventions where they talk about how socialism and four-letter words are ruining the country."

Terrizi had picked up the word Florida. If the Hampters had had a house there, Georgina would be apt to know oleander.

". . . Zora could get a secretarial job easy, but that way she wouldn't have much time to herself daytimes, for her own work."

Terrizi asked how the play was coming. Sergeant Bayles sighed. "This is the eighth draft she's working on now, and I've already read the first seven. I think I'm developing a reader's block. You and Angie want to go bowling with us Monday night? When's Angie's night off now?"

Terrizi said Angie had been put on the daytime shift at the answering service. "Simplifies my love life considerably. I'll ask her about Monday night. If I'm not still on the Dilman case."

"I knew it was a case as soon as Mrs. Ramsdale phoned and left a message for the inspector. Something about an alibi for Jeff Solent. What gives?"

Terrizi brought his colleague up to date. "But don't spill any of this to Zora."

"Never again." Bayles's smile flashed brilliantly in his dark face. "I'll be like that three-hundred-pound dame in England who had her teeth cemented together."

"We'll break the news to Georgina Hampter—if it's news—and see how she reacts. We're going there next."

"She's gone out to some meeting. Zora told me. And wait'll you hear what Hampter's been doing this morning. She copied out a lot of passages from those books before she heaved them down the incinerator, and now . . ."

"If I hadn't gone over there last night and involved Lawrence Dilman in all this mess, he wouldn't be dead." Marcy Coving's eyes and nose were pinkish from crying, but to Jeff Solent this didn't make her too repulsive. "I knew he had a bad heart, but I just didn't think."

"You aren't thinking now. You're emoting." Even more than a slap on the face to cure hysteria, Solent believed that to accuse a modern woman of emoting was powerful instant therapy.

Certainly it had a bracing effect on Marcy. Instead of going on dabbing with a handkerchief, she blew her nose in a decisive, trumpeting way, to herald an announcement: "I am not emoting." Pear-shaped vowels, clearly executed. "But when the Associated Press man told me Georgina Hampter had backed down on her promise, it seemed all the more terrible if Lawrence Dilman died for nothing. And I made up my mind what I'd do."

"Join Eldridge Cleaver in Algeria?"

"I'm tired of your stupid cracks."

"I'm only witty in stimulating company."

"Then go see that fat old actress. You seemed to be having an uproariously stimulating time with her at dinner last night."

"I was. Which reminds me." He pulled something out of his pants pocket. "I forgot to give her this after I found it in—"

"Do you or don't you want to hear what I've decided to do?"

"I do." He sounded relatively meek, and he put whatever it was on the table beside him. He also kicked off his sneakers and flexed his bare toes. "Spill."

"I'm going to replace those books in the library. Right away."

"All of them? I never doubted you'd replace Dilman's *Wayward the World*."

"Even the Hampter woman thinks that should be de-banned. 'Out of respect for the dead,' the AP man told me. But that's not enough. Lawrence Dilman spent his last evening—practically his last hour alive—to persuade her to drop the whole crazy censorship thing."

"He didn't persuade her. He twisted her arm till she went down on her knees and groveled."

"That's not true. He simply made her see how wrong and irrational she was."

"So the minute he's dead she finds she was right all along."

"How can you say she's right?"

"I didn't say *I* thought she was right. I said *she* thought so. You read her statement on filth. Women like that dig for would-be dirt the way a pig digs for truffles. That's a good line. I'll use it in class."

"You can write me a postcard and tell me how it goes over. If you have my next address."

For the first time, Jeff looked alarmed. He stopped poking at whatever he'd put on the table and concentrated on Marcy. "Where are you going?"

"Who knows? It's awfully late to land a job for next fall. I'll write out a Job Wanted thing for the *Library Monthly* now, before Georgina gets me fired. If nothing comes through, I'll manage somehow." She sounded self-consciously brave.

"You could always move in with me. I could sleep on the sofa the way they did in old movies. Whenever

134

you heard a thud in the night, you'd have to come pick me up off the floor and cradle me in your arms and croon the 'Lullaby of Broadway.'"

Marcy sniffed. "I'd rather baby-sit for a living."

"Too many husbands would stay home with the sitter."

"You're a great one to worry about protecting my virtue."

"I wasn't thinking of your virtue. I was thinking of the husbands. Look what you did to Lawrence Dilman last night."

Forty seconds later he was shouting through the locked bathroom door, "I did *not* mean you gave him a heart attack. That had nothing to do with you."

The bathroom, like the bedroom, opened off the tiny living room, and Jeff, addressing his locked-in love, was not only visible but highly audible through the screen door as the inspector and Terrizi came up on the porch.

"Say something." Jeff was pounding on the bathroom door now. "You can't cut your wrists with an electric razor." He put his ear against the door: deafening silence. "Do you want that Hampter woman to take over the school without even a fight? She's already rid of Dilman. If you have any guts, you'll stop sniveling and replace those books. You should have replaced them yesterday. No, Monday is better. I'll cancel my classes and take you in to New York myself."

He finally wound down enough to be aware of the doorbell zzz-ing. He turned, recognized Sergeant Terrizi, and shouted, "Marcy, the police are here!"

His lover's ear caught the answering murmur. "No, it's not a trick. Come out and see for yourself, or they'll have to break down the door and then your landlady will be sore."

To the callers, he bellowed, with unnecessary volume, "Come in."

The inspector, conditioned by obsolete imagery, had expected to interview a middle-aged woman with arch preservers; he had been further misled by Sergeant Terrizi's muttering on the porch, "The librarian's crazy kid."

In a low tone, he said to Solent, "How long ago did your mother lock herself in?"

Jeff Solent staggered against the wall, laughing wildly. "Marcy, he thinks you're my mother. Now you'll *have* to show." He said loudly, "Actually, she's not my mother, she's my maiden aunt. Sergeant, tell her you're here with a detective or something."

The scandalized Terrizi said, "This is Inspector McDougal with me, Miss Coving."

"Oh." Pause. "Just a minute." Soon there was a clunky sound as a bolt was pulled back.

Marcy Coving emerged, looking as unlike a maiden aunt as is possible on short notice. She had used at least the latter part of her stay in the bathroom to powder the pinkish disaster areas and put on fresh lipstick (not Lotus Lick but a last year's tint called Deviled Ham), and she had combed her pale yellow hair. Her costume was as before: blue jeans and a white sweat shirt which had shrunk enough so it did not have that baggy shapelessness one frequently gets in sweat shirts.

The sergeant, sneaking a glance at his superior, was gratified to see McDougal's usually firm jaw hanging loose. "This is Miss Coving, the high school librarian . . . Inspector McDougal."

Miss Coving shook hands with a pleasant, professional smile; she had the cool of an oyster on ice. "Inspector, Sergeant, do sit down. I'm sorry Jeff subjected you to this ridiculous scene."

"*I* subjected them?"

"You've said enough."

"I haven't said anything yet. I'm Jeff Solent, Inspector. And if you've come here about Miss Coving's visit to the Dilmans' last night, I can tell you right now she was acting as a conscientious librarian determined to prevent reactionaries like Georgina Hampter from—"

"Jeff! These gentlemen came to see me." The *gentlemen* was meanly underlined, along with the *me*. "You'd better go."

Solent went back to his chair and sat down. He also folded his arms and waggled his moustache in a manner meant to be formidable. "I want to know why they're here, and I intend to make sure you aren't bullied."

The inspector said, "Miss Coving doesn't look like a candidate for the third degree. Besides, it's officially frowned on."

"She's got this idiotic guilt thing about Dilman's death. I've told her and told her that Georgina Hampter's responsible."

"Are you accusing Mrs. Hampter of murder?"

"Good God, no! She'd sue the pants off me. Anyway, it isn't a question of murder. The guy died of a heart attack."

"As it happens, he didn't. He was poisoned."

Solent let out his breath in a sharp whistling sound. Marcy Coving looked stupefied.

"Miss Coving, did Dilman seem all right when he started dinner?"

Marcy was very pale and her eyes looked enormous, but she managed to keep her voice steady. "He was fine then. He wanted my advice about cataloging his own library, and he asked me if I'd work on it this summer." She avoided looking at Jeff, which was just as well; his scowl was horrendous.

"Did you say you would?"

"I said I'd let him know later, that I had to consult a friend about vacation plans."

Jeff's scowl was less fierce now.

"When did Dilman first act sick? After he drank the wine?"

"It was after he started eating—I'd say five or six minutes after. He complained that the shish kebab was lousy. I thought it was just because he'd had several drinks and had got to the picky stage. Mrs. Terrizi heard him when she served the salad, and she banged down the—" Marcy stopped abruptly.

Terrizi said, "Don't worry about me, Miss Coving. I've known Mama for twenty-three years plus womb time."

"I didn't blame her for being cross. After she'd waited so long to serve dinner. And she'd remembered to leave the tomato off his skewer, and—"

"You heard Mrs. Dilman give the instructions about no tomato?"

"Oh, yes. But I knew it couldn't have been tomato that made him sick because there wasn't even a tiny piece on his shish kebab."

"Did he go on complaining?"

"He—he said—I don't think it has anything to do with what you want to know."

"Tell us and we'll decide."

She still hesitated.

"It was something about his wife?"

She looked unhappy. "Yes, but he couldn't have meant it, because when he got really sick he turned to Mrs. Dilman right away. She was the only one he wanted."

"He said she fed him all the wrong things and that she'd insisted on having shish kebab. That was it, wasn't it?"

Marcy nodded.

"Did you go out to the greenhouse at any time?" She seemed puzzled by the switch. "No."

"Mr. Solent. How about you?"

"Sure I went to the greenhouse. What the hell does that have to do with anything? If you mean did I snitch a can of deadly nicotine bug spray—" He made a disgusted noise. "Too corny."

"Some of the best murder methods are corny. But Alison Moffat has given you an alibi. She called headquarters and left a message that you were with her every minute of that time before dinner."

Solent said in an odd tone, "Oh? That's nice of her. She's a great old girl." He groped for something on the table. "Where the hell did I put my lighter?" His hand went into his pants pocket and wriggled in search. "Must have left it at home. No, here it is." He flicked the lighter twice before remembering to get out a cigarette. "Did the poison really come from the greenhouse?"

"We think so. And we're trying to pinpoint the people who would have had a chance to get it before dinner. Say, an hour before."

"Mrs. Hampter went to the greenhouse about that time," Marcy said. "Mr. Dilman had persuaded her to apologize to me for taking the books from the library. And she promised to drop the whole thing. That was on the terrace. Then Barbara Dilman invited her to go out to the greenhouse, but I'm quite sure she went alone because Mrs. Dilman had to go look for briquets or something instead."

McDougal nodded. "We saw Mrs. Dilman

briefly this morning, and she says the same thing. Did her husband offer to show you his oleander? It's quite spectacular."

Marcy flushed. "He did say something about going out with him to see the orchids, or maybe it was some other plant, but I thought—well, it was so close to dinnertime—"

"What she thought," Jeff Solent said, "was that Dilman was trying a variation of the old come-roll-in-my-art-collection routine."

Marcy Coving tried to protest, but Solent talked faster and louder. "Dilman was prancing around like a drunken goat. He'd have chased Marcy round and round the oleander bush, if she'd had enough wits left to run."

"You saw the bush when you were in the greenhouse with Alison Moffat?"

"Sure I saw the bush. I couldn't care less about that tropical stuff. I got a bellyful in Vietnam. A guy in the Medical Corps told us—" He broke off abruptly, warily. "I'm beginning to see light at the end of the trap."

"You sharpened the last few skewers for the shish kebab?"

"Of maple," Solent said, very clearly. "Not oleander."

"Did you cut the branches off a tree yourself? Or did somebody hand you a stick and you sharpened it?"

"Joan—that's Dilman's daughter—gave me one, but I know damn well it was maple. I saw her cut it. There's a clump of small maples right behind that outdoor fireplace."

"What knife did you and Miss Dilman use?"

"She got it from the greenhouse." His head jerked up. "And if you're thinking that's how she switched the skewers, you're barking up the wrong bush. She wasn't in there more than a minute."

"You *did* notice the bush when you and Miss Moffat were in the greenhouse later?"

"Yeah—vaguely. Not to examine it." Solent put out a half-smoked cigarette with elaborate care but instantly lit another. "If I were you, I'd give Georgina Hampter the third degree on that. She was in there first. And she's the one who hated Dilman's guts. He had something on her."

"That's only Jeff's opinion." Marcy sounded condescending.

Terrizi stirred and opened his mouth to speak; the inspector could almost see the words about to burst from between the sergeant's strong front teeth: Mama and Mrs. Ramsdale thought the same thing.

To forestall any such indiscretion—this seemed to be the sergeant's day for talking too much on duty—McDougal said, "I'll keep it in mind when I see Mrs. Hampter."

Solent said, "As soon as Dilman was dead, Hampter reneged on her promise. But Marcy's going to buy new books next week anyway. Even if she gets fired for it." Solent was looking at the girl as if he'd just invented her and found his work good.

"I hope it won't come to that." The inspector made a mental note to have another talk with Chief Salter. The Hampter woman might or might not have killed Dilman, but she had certainly been guilty of destroying school property. Even in Wingate, the police should be able to do something.

One member of the police force was already doing something, in an unofficial way. ". . . and I just happened to hear," Terrizi was telling Marcy Coving, "that the Hampter dame's getting up a flyer to distribute all over town, quoting all the dirty passages from those books—I mean, what she calls dirty."

"Listen, Marcy, why don't we get up a flyer of our own, quoting dirty passages from the Bible?"

"The school board wouldn't be amused. Three of the members are still fighting to get prayers put back in the curriculum."

"You know the one I was taught by a cook of ours when I was a kid?" Jeff said. " 'If I should die before I wake, I pray the Lord my soul to take.' Scared the bejesus out of me. I used to lie awake nights to make sure I was still alive. Poor old Dilman, his soul's up for grabs right now. 'At stroke of midnight, God will win'—like hell."

Marcy gave him a wait-till-I-get-you-alone look.

Solent said, "OK, so maybe he's chasing the best-looking angel in the choir. Have they done an autopsy? Is that how you knew about the oleander?"

The mention of an autopsy made Marcy quiver. "If you men say one more thing about oleander without explaining," she said, in a small, tight voice, "I'll start screaming."

"Ignorance is bliss." Solent had his hand in his pocket again. "Isn't that right, inspector?"

Bitterness and exhaustion washed over McDougal like a tidal wave. "Miss Coving might be pretending. Women are good at that."

In the police car a few minutes later, McDougal said, "Hell of an example I set for you, just now. Thanks for getting us out of there fast." His throat and mouth felt painfully dry, and he had to push out the words. "I'd better get off the case."

Terrizi swerved the car to miss a youngster on a wobbly bicycle. "Without you, there wouldn't have been a case. Nobody would have figured out that oleander gimmick. Your getting back here in time was real luck."

"Luck," the inspector said bleakly.

"For me, it was luck. And you've taught me more in the last two years than any police academy could in a lifetime."

McDougal was deeply moved. He wanted to say something generous—*You're a born cop. . . . Working with you has meant a lot to me*—but that sort of thing was difficult for him at any time, and all the more now, when his emotions were caught in barbed wire.

The police short-wave radio crackled with a call for the inspector.

"McDougal here."

The voice became less official, and Sergeant Bayles's lilt crept in. "Inspector, Mrs. Ramsdale said, tell you she'll be out this afternoon but she wants to see you around six. She says she has something important to tell you."

McDougal felt suddenly, rather cheerfully, lightheaded. "Did she say she'd feed me too?"

Sergeant Bayles's deep, rich chuckle rolled back. "Yes, sir. She said you'd have to interview the lady who's visiting her, so you might as well eat while you're there. I think she's rounding up a steer."

"She's very good with a lasso."

This time there was no lilt. "You mean I should tell her no if she calls back?"

"I'll try to see her at six."

Lilt again. "Yes, sir. I'll tell her. Over and out."

"The fatted calf, medium rare," McDougal said, a few minutes later. But he sounded quite amiable.

This emboldened Terrizi to say, "I sure could use a hamburger."

"We might as well eat now."

Terrizi drove on contentedly, humming a TV commercial. *It takes two hands to handle a whopper.* . . . Hands . . . something about hands that he'd intended to ask McDougal as soon as they left Marcy Coving's apartment. He scrambled through his mind and retrieved what he wanted. "Did you see Solent palm something from the table beside him?"

The inspector shook his head. He found it quite easy to say, "This wasn't my brightest morning. All I noticed was that Solent acted skittish when I told him he'd been given an alibi. Wait a minute. Solent began groping for his lighter then. Is that when he slid something off the table?"

"That's it."

"Any idea what he palmed?"

"No, but I heard something when he put his hand in his pocket."

"You sure it wasn't loose change jingling?"

Terrizi looked rather embarrassed but determined. "It was more like a teensy bird going *tweet-tweet.*"

# 13

Lucy's guest had done that infuriating thing—said, "I want to hear all about everything"—and then taken the conversation between her teeth and run away with it. This is aggravating enough when a friend says, "I want to hear all about your trip," and then tells all about hers instead. But in Lucy's case, with the murder fresh on her tongue, it was all the more maddening because Alison talked mostly about Jeff Solent: Jeff wanted her to tape scenes from several of her plays to use in his classes; Jeff thought she should do a TV play, a comedy, "not one of those dreadful series—wholesome manure sprinkled with pumpkin seeds. He thinks they're desperately in need of my kind of comedy—high style, understated." One of Jeff's Yale Drama School classmates was in educational television, and Jeff wanted to arrange a session with Alison and his friend in New York. . . .

Whenever Lucy managed to ram a few lines of her own into this monologue, Alison would short-circuit her.

"You must have noticed that oleander plant when you were in the greenhouse with Solent."

145

"We were too busy talking to go around sniffing dainty white blossoms. That boy should be a drama critic. I'm going to talk to Doug Brill. Doug must have been pleased to hear about Larry this morning."

"Jeff Solent must have been even happier. It was his girl Larry was trying to take over."

"Jeff wasn't concerned in the least. He knew Marcy was just being kind to an old man."

"You told me yourself on the terrace you wanted to go calm Jeff down. He hurtled off like a thunderbolt."

"He'd forgotten the whole silly thing by the time I got to him."

"I can't understand why you didn't run into Georgina Hampter if you took Jeff right over to the greenhouse. You might have caught her in the act, whacking a branch off that plant."

"Fragrante delicto." Alison glinted with pleasure over her pun.

Lucy wasn't amused. "Do you know what time you and Jeff went over there? If we could narrow it down—"

"Those minute-by-minute timetables in detective stories are always so boring. And I wasn't wearing a watch." She flung up her right arm, and her kimono sleeve caught on her bracelet. While she was trying to unsnag it, she suddenly muttered, "My charm's gone."

At first, Lucy thought her guest meant this in the larger social sense—"I'm not fun to be with any more" —and was privately inclined to agree. But when Alison twirled her bracelet around her wrist, to examine each dangle, and wailed, "I've lost one," Lucy watched as long as she could stand it, then snapped, "If you insist on loading yourself like a Christmas tree with junk jewelry—" She scooped up the breakfast tray and marched out to the kitchen.

She could hear Alison's footsteps slap-slapping up the stairs in the dreadful house slippers. They sounded slower, older somehow, and Lucy's irritation evaporated. Poor darling, the news about Larry really shook her. That's why she couldn't bear to listen; she had to keep babbling on. It's not an actress's fault if she turns real grief into a performance. Writers turn it into a book; actors have to act it out. Even if she was cured of Larry, she had to sit there last night and watch him making an idiot of himself over a young girl.

Now the wasted English muffin on the breakfast plate seemed pathetic. Lucy carried the crumbled bits out to the bird feeder behind the house and thought of the time Hal had hung the first feeder there, from the maple tree, so that she could see the birds while she was working at the kitchen sink. If Alison had had a husband like Hal—but she couldn't have got him in the first place, and she couldn't have held him. I was so much luckier.

Lucy didn't have to tell herself *and lovelier and gayer and more charming;* she simply knew it. From this pleasant vantage of superiority, she could afford to feel so forgiving she vowed she'd make up for her bad temper and her crack about junk jewelry. For lunch, she'd do the clam casserole and little cheese biscuits. . . .

It was diddling, messy work to cut up the clams and the green and red peppers. The dish looked rather *Ladies' Home Journal*-ish—all those red and green bits like confetti—but it didn't taste itsy. She was rolling Ritz crackers for the crumb topping when her guest appeared in the same suit she'd worn when she'd got off the train the day before. She seemed to be in sparkling spirits. "Darling, Jeff Solent called and asked me to have lunch with him at the Inn. I knew you wouldn't mind."

Her hostess seethed. You mean you didn't give a damn whether I'd mind or not. It wouldn't occur to you that I might enjoy a lunch out too: cooking myself into a frazzle, to fix meals you don't even eat. . . . She thought of saying, Then perhaps you'd like to hire another limousine tonight and take me to the Bird & Bottle for dinner (it was the most expensive place she could think of offhand). But she remembered just in time that McDougal might be home then. She said, "Have fun with your juvenile lead."

Alison actually giggled. "He's picking me up at one, so I'll just walk down the driveway now—then he needn't come up to the house." This was even more insulting, as if Lucy would corner that juvenile and invite herself to make a third.

"If you plan to stay out for dinner too, you might let me know ahead."

It was icy sarcasm, but Alison said, "Oh, I wouldn't miss meeting your inspector at dinner."

Doesn't mind being a third herself, Lucy thought, after all her palaver earlier about being in the way here. But as soon as Alison left, Lucy had a horrifying preview of dinner: the table set for three; Alison all primed; McDougal no show. On top of the snub about lunch, this prospect was absolutely unthinkable. The inspector must not only appear, but she, Lucy, must be featured as his valued colleague.

At that point, she had phoned police headquarters and left the message for McDougal. The "I have someting important to tell him," was primeval bait, but Lucy had every intention of backing it up with a solid hook.

She put the clam casserole into the freezer and made herself a tomato, lettuce, and mayonnaise sandwich which she ate absentmindedly, dribbling into two paper napkins, while she considered her next move. If Larry Dilman had had something on Georgina, it must have been something that happened in Wingate. And if it had happened in Wingate, then there had certainly been talk. There was never fire without smoke in this town; the gossip billowed in smoky clouds even before two sticks rubbed together. But then why hadn't she heard about it herself? The back room of the Second Run Thrift Shop where she and other volunteers sorted the donations to be resold for the benefit of the District Nursing Association was one of the most productive gossip marts in town. A volunteer checking the lining on a slightly mangy mink cape would say, "Dotty's husband bought her this right after he took his secretary to the convention in Chicago. He'd told her a wife wasn't a business deduction on a trip and that all the secretaries stayed at the YWCA, but Dotty had a friend check the register at the Blackstone Hotel...."

The parking lot behind the Thrift Shop was jammed that Saturday afternoon. Lucy nosed her little Saab into a space between a Honda and a station wagon the length of a hearse and went in through the rear entrance. A sign tacked on the back door read: PLEASE LEAVE ALL MERCHANDISE IN HALLWAY WITH YOUR NAME AND ADDRESS FIRMLY ATTACHED. The hallway was empty except for a small, scarred chest of drawers and a tricycle missing a tire. Judging from the babble of voices inside—it sounded like the birdhouse at the Central Park Zoo—quite a few donors had managed to penetrate the inner circle bearing gifts and hoping for a tidbit of gossip. Her first glimpse of the back room confirmed this: plus the four volunteers (all golf widows) normally on duty, who were emptying cartons and sorting the contents in laundry baskets, there were at least eight or ten ladies perched on unopened cartons or standing in clumps, chattering. She barely had time to hear, "Barbara Dilman had him sign that will before . . ." which sounded promising, when one of the golf widows spotted her. "Lucy! Thank God you've come. The shop's been so mobbed all day we're running out of stock. Will you take a look out front and let us know what they're low on?"

This wasn't at all what Lucy had had in mind, but she'd been a conscientious volunteer long enough to leap to emergencies. Casing the long front room—the shop proper—with an experienced eye, she saw that the rack of maternity clothes was bare and that three or four young women with swelling fronts were adrift. Having been frustrated in what they came for, they were still buy-minded; one was examining a hideous bronze Cupid, another was fingering an almost complete set of hollow-stemmed champagne glasses, and a third was eyeing a Seth Thomas clock that didn't run.

Lucy stuck her head into the back room, to give an S.O.S. for maternity reinforcements, and waved to the harassed woman at the cash register. This was Laura Stebble, the only paid worker, and paid so little she might well have been called a three-quarter volunteer. "Lucy, will you check on the formals?" she said—actually, she had to yell to make herself heard above the clatter of the cash register and the customers—and then something else about "selling like crazy . . . Junior Prom."

Lucy headed for the alcove that had once housed millinery and now announced, on its placard: JEWELRY, EVENING WEAR. Below this sign was another, evidently printed in a hurry: MOTHERS!! KEEP YOUR CHILDREN AWAY FROM THIS SECTION—PLEASE! YOU WILL BE HELD RESPONSIBLE FOR THEIR ACTIONS.

The youngest child here at the moment was around sixteen, lanky, with hanks of stringy hair; she was standing before the full-length mirror holding up a gold sequin dress, a John Held Junior-ish number. It looked especially piquant against her blue jeans. "Hi, Mrs. Ramsdale. I spent most of my clothes allowance on feed for my horse. Oats are horribly expensive now, and all I have left is—I can't find a price tag on this dress. Could you tell me how much it is?"

Lucy, who knew the child's mother, Polly Evans, another Thrift Shop volunteer, guessed what was left of the clothes allowance and said, "Four dollars." She quieted her conscience by telling herself she could make up the difference the next time she put a price tag on one of the popular antiques such as a hand-painted chamberpot.

The child looked at herself in the mirror again and frowned. "This is the only thing my size, but I was thinking of—you know, like a granny gown—long, with puff sleeves. My boy friend's going to wear a Civil War uniform he found here, and this might not look right with his outfit."

The only other dresses left on the rack were a drooping elephant-colored velvet and a black-fringed crepe with rhinestone shoulder straps. "Mummy said if I didn't find what I wanted, there might be some better ones in the back room."

Lucy said she'd look. "If you have any errands to do, come back in a half hour and I'll see what I can dig up."

"I'll go to the Hungry Bear for a Coke and get some more signatures on my petition." She reached behind the large sign propped on a glass display case—DO NOT OPEN YOURSELF! ASK CASHIER TO SHOW YOU COSTUME JEWELRY—and extracted a clipboard with a yellow pencil dangling from a string. "Mummy said not to tackle anybody in here because it's against the law or something for a charity organization to take sides. She told Daddy and me at lunch about the time you brought in a petition and made customers sign so Mrs. Hampter wouldn't get reelected to the school board. Mummy said it made a lot of people furious, but I thought it was neat. Would you like to see ours?"

Lucy, without her reading glasses, had to hold the clipboard at arm's length. WE THE UNDERSIGNED NEVER LIVED IN NAZI GERMANY WHEN THEY BURNED BOOKS BEFORE THEY BURNED JEWS. AND STUDENTS IN WINGATE ARE NOT HITLER JUGEND—SO LET THEM READ AND THINK FOR THEMSELVES.

Lucy said she thought it was marvelous.

"Mr. Solent helped us write it. He's the librarian's boy friend."

"I met them last night at the Dilmans' just before Larry had his attack." She had been waiting to tell this in the back room, but she couldn't resist the preliminary run-through.

"I know," the child said casually. "It's all over town. Mummy's been yakking on the phone for hours. She and Mr. Dilman worked on the Bicentennial Committee ages ago, and Mummy said Mr. Dilman charmed the pants off all the biddies—even Georgina Hampter."

Lucy felt a leap of excitement. The Wingate Bicentennial! She and Hal had spent most of that year in France, so she wouldn't have heard any gossip about it.

"I think all those patriotic celebrations are crud," the Evans child was saying. "They make gassy speeches about 'our glorious freedoms' and then they go out and burn books."

Lucy disliked red-white-and-blue hoopla, but she felt a perverse need to defend her country. "Georgina

Hampter's not typical. She's just a stupid white-collar red-neck."

"Well, plenty of people around here agree with her. Even Mummy had a fit when I brought home the Eldridge Cleaver. I told her that parents ought to stop thinking of their own childhood—I mean, what was OK to read then—and think of their children instead. If the kids can't read those books, we won't be prepared for what's happening in the world." Her thin young voice went up in almost a wail. "We have to know."

Lucy felt a surge of affection, "Of course you do. And I want to sign your petition right now."

"Wow, would you? Maybe we should go outside so Mummy won't get into a sweat."

There was something especially endearing about a revolutionary who protected her mother's sensibilities.

"I'll duck behind the clothes rack." Lucy signed her name in her large, uphill scrawl and underlined it with a flourish.

The youngster retrieved the clipboard and examined it with satisfaction. "Mostly I've only been able to get kids to sign. Now maybe I can get some of the other old people—not that you're old, Mrs. Ramsdale. I mean, you don't act old. You think more like somebody my age."

"God forbid," Lucy said. "I wouldn't be your age again for anything in the world. And when your generation makes a hero out of some psycho cop-killer I could whack the whole lot of you." She had fire in her eye.

The Evans child backed toward the door. "I don't really go for the killing bit. And if you come across some more dresses, Mrs. Ramsdale. . . ."

On her way to the back room, Lucy had to direct several customers to Children's Underwear (in bins, by sizes and sex) and convince another woman that the chip in the Spode soup tureen really didn't show—much —and that if it weren't for that tiny flaw, the price wouldn't be $3.25.

By the time she reached the back room, the gaggle of extras had been shooed away and the regulars were settling down with a cup of tea. Lucy got herself a paper cup from the dispenser, put in a teaspoonful of instant tea, squeezed a lemon-shaped plastic object for a squirt of acid flavor, and poured boiling water from a kettle on the electric hot plate. The sign above it bristled with exclamation points: BE SURE! PULL CORD FROM OUTLET! LET'S NOT BURN DOWN THE BUILDING. A philanthropic merchant had loaned the small one-story building rent free, so this was a decent precaution.

Lucy didn't pull the plug because the volunteers might want refills. Not that they knocked off for tea; they could sip, work, and gossip at the same time, which men find more baffling than patting one's head and rubbing one's stomach simultaneously. Two of the golf widows had a large carton between them and were hauling out maternity dresses.

"Hilda Miller brought these in right after she had her fourth. She had her tubes tied while she was in the hospital—"

Normally, Hilda Miller would have got a more thorough going-over, but Lucy cut off Hilda and her tubes ruthlessly. "Who do we know besides Polly Evans who worked on the Wingate two-hundredth-anniversary thing?"

"You know me." The oldest golf widow, Liz Carmody, who was shaped rather like a golf ball herself, smoothed the front panel of a chocolate-brown maternity dress and slid it onto a hanger. "I was thinking this morning when I heard about Lawrence Dilman—the members of that committee are dying off like fruit flies. Margaret Osgood this spring and Cass Williams two years ago, and now Georgina Hampter's acting so weird they'll probably have to lock her up."

Her partner on the other side of the carton sniffed. "Georgina is *not* acting crazy at all." Her nose quivered like a rabbit's. "She had to take things into her own hands because nobody else had the courage. I'll tell you who is acting crazy: it's the teachers who shove that disgusting filth into students' minds. And I know for a fact the high school librarian is sleeping with a teacher right out in the open."

"On the village green?" Lucy said. "Or in a cornfield? Marcy Coving's a nice intelligent girl, and I can't see what the hell business of ours it is who she sleeps with."

"As long as the man is single," another volunteer said placidly. "Remember the mess when the geometry teacher left his wife and six children and ran away with a waitress at the Hungry Bear?"

The Hungry Bear reminded Lucy of her promise to Polly Evans's daughter. "Has anybody brought in some evening dresses we haven't unpacked?"

The jump from Hungry Bear to evening dresses didn't faze her listeners in the slightest.

"Margaret Osgood's daughter just finished cleaning out that huge old house, and she came in Thursday with some lovely things of Margaret's. I put the boxes back in a corner till—" Liz Carmody didn't have to say till *what*. All the ladies could supply the rest of the thought instantly: till I had a chance to see if there was anything my daughter-in-law in California could use. They all practiced it, with variations, on special goodies, but most of them bent over backwards to charge themselves a fair price.

They watched with ladylike greed as Liz tugged a large carton over to the group, untied the cord, and began to haul out the contents. Lucy never wore secondhand clothes; she had had her fill of that in the Depression, when the hand-me-downs of a well-to-do aunt were cut down to fit her size ten figure. She was still a size ten. And she was greedy now only in an altruistic way, because the Evans child had handed her what might be the pure gold link between Larry Dilman and Georgina. "That pink brocade with puffed sleeves," she said. "Toss it over, will you?"

This did surprise the ladies; Lucy Ramsdale had never been the pink-puffed-sleeves type. They looked at each other covertly, worriedly. "I remember when Margaret wore that," Liz Carmody said. "At the Bicentennial Ball. She gained so much weight she probably never wore it again. It was a bit too girlish for her even then."

Lucy didn't seem to take the gentle hint. "Is four dollars all right for this?"

This too seemed unlike Lucy—on the stingy side—but the others agreed politely.

"Polly Evans's daughter needs it for the prom. She spent her clothes allowance on feed for her horse."

Her listeners looked relieved. Lucy wasn't going into the pink-puffed-sleeves stage, which often precedes round spots of rouge on both cheeks.

"Polly was pregnant when she was on our committee," Liz Carmody said. "So that child must be seventeen. How time gallops. Speaking of gallops, I think we should get a local ordinance to keep horses off the paved roads. It's bad enough when they're ridden, but when they run around loose...."

The ladies discussed a member of the horsy set who

was also running around loose. "She sold her horse so she could have an excuse to rent from the Wilson Stables and she and that riding instructor know every back road from here to Danbury. They tie up their horses . . . and she had the nerve to tell somebody they were in the woods looking for arbutus!"

Lucy was barely listening; she was impatient to talk to Liz Carmody alone, and she suggested, a bit bossily, that the others take whatever maternity clothes they had ready out front to the shop. "Oh, I can carry these few things myself," Liz's partner said. "The rest of you go ahead on Margaret Osgood's boxes."

Lucy took the woman's seat as soon as she'd left and pulled the chair closer to Liz. "Was Georgina Hampter horribly difficult to work with on the committee? I should think she and Larry Dilman would have fought like fury."

"Larry knew how to handle her. He called her Georgie Porgie and Gorgeous Georgie—she was quite good looking in those days. Of course, she was reactionary even then. I remember Larry wanted to use a quote from Thomas Paine on a placard, and Georgina said Paine was no better than a Communist agitator. A funny thing, I was reading last month in *American Heritage* that Paine was an *Englishman*. I always thought he was one of our great American patriots."

"Well, most of them came from England," Lucy said absently. "Did Larry persuade Georgina to let him have his way?"

"Didn't he always, with the ladies? No matter what he suggested after that, Georgina seemed to go along. I think it did her good to be kidded and flattered and unknotted a bit. The night of the ball she looked absolutely smashing. You know the way women look when

157

they're in love—sort of phosphorescent, as if they'd glow in the dark? But I always thought her husband was made of building blocks. What a square."

"Was Larry at the ball?"

"Was he ever! We had a Paul Jones or whatever that thing is when you change partners, and even I got a chance to dance with him." She gazed into space dreamily, and then her eyes sharpened. "Let me see that black lace dress. Margaret only bought it last winter...."

The volunteer who had opened the second carton gathered Margaret's black lace to her large bosom. "I get first dibs."

Bunch of ghouls, Lucy thought, but amiably. She had got what she'd come for—and more. In a peacemaking gesture, she murured to Liz, "It's too matronly for you anyway. Let her have it."

The volunteer who had lugged the maternity clothes out to the shop was now untying the third carton. She thrust in her hand. "Feels like a fur jacket." She went on groping and suddenly screamed. "It's got a head!"

Lucy sat frozen. She remembered with horrible clarity the time she'd opened a bin here and found a body.

"It's got two heads," the woman wailed.

Lucy relaxed. No corpse had two heads.

"Oh, I bet I know what that is," Liz Carmody said. While the other volunteer shrank back, Liz reached in and hauled out a three-foot-high fuzzy grayish-white creature. It *did* have two heads, both of them glassy eyed.

"Margaret's husband had the lamb stuffed," Liz said. "It was born on their farm and got to be quite a pet. But what the hell can we do with it?"

Lucy said, "Put it in a glass display case with a sign: GOOD-LUCK MASCOT—HEADS YOU WIN. Price it high, fifteen or twenty dollars, and it will sell like a breeze for somebody's family room. We'll be getting requests for two-headed lambs all summer."

The other ladies accepted this advice gratefully, although one of them did say, "But where would we get more two-headed lambs?"

It was then almost three o'clock. Lucy attached a tag—HOLD FOR EVANS—to the pink dress with puffed sleeves and hoped the Evans child would consider it in the granny gown category. A good thing Margaret Osgood had been skinny then.

The remainder of Margaret's third carton turned up three more evening dresses which Lucy said she'd leave in the shop, with the pink brocade, on her way out. Liz Carmody went along, ostensibly to help carry.

In the crowded front room, as they were hanging the clothes on the rack in the alcove, Liz muttered, "Did somebody bump off Larry Dilman? Is that why you were picking my brains?"

"Inspector McDougal doesn't want me to say anything right now, so keep that idea to yourself."

Liz Carmody rushed back to her fellow volunteers in a flush of achievement, to report that Larry Dilman had been murdered and Lucy Ramsdale's inspector was working on the case with Lucy. "And you must keep this to yourselves, girls. They don't want any talk right now." These admonitions to secrecy were the sort of thing that kept the Wingate grapevine lushly green and growing.

Lucy, buoyed by her own sense of achievement and euphoric to boot, was in Coleman's Market around the corner from the Thrift Shop, consulting with Jack the butcher. Years before, she and her husband had dubbed him Jack the Ripper as a family joke. With inflation, their friends had picked up the nickname, not altogether jokingly. Coleman's prices were wicked, and constantly getting wickeder, but their meats were almost worth it. And for Lucy, a favorite customer, Jack the Ripper, presiding in his blood-stained apron, would cut off the fat before he weighed the meat.

She had decided on steak à poivre for dinner; while Jack was in the back room cutting up prime beef, Lucy leaned against the Cold Meats section and remembered the first time she'd met the inspector, right in this spot. He had been prickly then; today he'd seemed even worse, but not so much prickly as hell-ridden. Whatever the ex-wife had done to him this time, it had been almost fatal.

With rare self-effacement, Lucy decided she would just give him the facts that pointed to Larry and Georgina's having some sort of affair seventeen years before. Let McDougal be the one to say, "It would give Dilman a handle for blackmail: 'Either you replace those books or—' and it would give Georgina a much stronger motive for killing him." Let Mac think he was figuring it all out by himself, and she would play dumb like Watson and exclaim over the brilliant deduction.

Driving home on Interstate 35, she was so bemused with this noble plan that a horse almost ran her down. It was a horse she knew, which made her even madder. It belonged to a family that had put up a rambling prefab house a half mile from Lucy's; they had three horses for five children and had built a high fence around the pasture bordering the road—but not high enough. This was a young horse, and it had cleared the top wooden bar easily and frisked across the road straight toward Lucy's car. Her brakes screeched just in time.

Liz Carmody was right: Wingate was getting impossible, between the Birchites acting like asses and the horses trying to hog the roads. . . . As the hoofs clattered past, she thought, We ought to get the Riding Club kids to pound around Wingate some night swinging lanterns and shouting, "The Book Burners are coming! The Book Burners are coming!"

She decided to suggest it to the Evans child. But if Georgina Hampter was arrested for murder, that ought to cool off the book burners—for a while.

# 14

"The knife has traces of oleander, all right. But the handle's a mess of smudges. They're trying to get a clear print."

The inspector could hear his voice saying the words, but he might have been listening to an actor playing cop in a banal TV series. The typed words in the lab reports had the same unreality.

Even Sergeant Terrizi, sitting four feet away on the other side of Chief Salter's desk, might have been a stranger who'd just happened in. The crackling black hair, the terra-cotta coloring, the bright, shiny look of a small boy fresh from his bath—McDougal noted all this in a tired, distant way. If anything, it made him feel tireder.

The sergeant, sensing the chasm, talked a bit too loudly and clearly, throwing out remarks as if he were throwing a rope to catch onto. "Mrs. Hampter's prints should be on file at headquarters. The Civil Defense people got almost everybody in town to come in and have their prints taken, for identification 'in case of nuclear incident.' If the lab comes up with even a partial, I'll run it through. But we wouldn't have Dilman's daughter or that lady visiting Mrs. Ramsdale. . . . We still haven't located the Dilmans' gardener, but he sure as hell wouldn't have hacked an oleander like that." He knew he was overstating the obvious, but it seemed important not to let silence take over. He was thinking, I shouldn't have gone home and left the inspector alone. He was doing OK before.

They had had lunch at the Hungry Bear ("No Dogs or Bare Feet Allowed") because it had the best sandwiches in Wingate. The inspector had eaten almost two thirds of his hamburger and hadn't seemed bothered by the squawk and yowl of young lunchers' transistor radios. This sign of at least partial recovery had sharpened Terrizi's own healthy appetite, and he'd longed to order a third burger for himself but was afraid under the circumstances it would seem piggish. Besides, McDougal wanted to get back to look over the latest lab reports.

According to Sergeant Bayles's girl, Mrs. Hampter wouldn't be home before five. And Zora had informed her fiancé that she'd decided to stay on the job a bit longer "because you cops need an undercover agent in here." Sergeant Bayles, grinning broadly, had told the others this as soon as they got back to headquarters. "Zora's papa voted for Nixon last time around, and she's trying to restore the balance of nature."

Terrizi had expected the inspector to fume, or even to issue a flat order: Zora was to get out of the Hampter house and stay clear. After all, if her employer was a murderer— But the inspector had actually looked amused. "Tell Zora if she can penetrate Citizens for a Clean-Minded Community and look over that list of dirty quotes, I'll give her a medal."

In this relatively jovial mood, he had urged Terrizi to go home for two hours. "Grab a nap and take a cold shower and get those twittering birds out of your head."

He had sweetened this by saying he'd go back to the studio for a nap himself, after he'd read the reports.

Now it seemed to the sergeant that McDougal hadn't gone anywhere except backward, into a slough of despond. (Terrizi's own summing up was, He's uptight again—bad as this morning.) The inspector's face was so taut and drawn it was as if his high cheekbones might pierce through the skin any minute. His eyes didn't have the glassiness of a drunk's: they were more like a blind man's.

In his concern, the sergeant blurted out, "You said you'd get some rest too. You need it more than me."

"I took a break and went back to the studio." McDougal remembered lying down on the bed, yawning: he had just plummeted into sleep when the phone blared. He had reached groggily for the receiver, expecting to hear the pathologist's voice, and instead he'd heard Eileen. . . .

Terrizi was saying, "I could have stayed here and gone over those reports for you." His eyes, as shiny black as ripe olives, were troubled.

"I wanted you to have a talk with your mother anyway. Could she give you some idea of the times she was out of the kitchen—say, from eight to nine? Or did she see anybody *in* the kitchen during that time, somebody who had no reason to be there?"

The sergeant longed to have something sensational to disclose, something to burst like a rocket and throw a brilliant illumination. He said in apology, "Mama was just leaving to go over to Mrs. Spolipsky's with a cake and some other stuff. Even a dog dies and Mama's gotta take food to the bereaved and stay for the wake. I tried to ask her some questions while I had her, but she said nobody was thinking about time last night, so why should she?"

The inspector nodded. He was staring over Terrizi's shoulder at a WANTED poster of a man with a dolichocephalic head and cup-handle ears, who was wanted for rape, armed robbery, and assaulting a police officer with a deadly weapon.

Terrizi said, loudly again, "Did you get the report on the autopsy of the dog?"

"Poison. Oleander. Same as Dilman's."

"Gee, that's great." He tried to think of something less geewhiz to say, something forceful and constructive. "The one thing Mama's sure of is that she saw Mrs. Hampter in the back hall after she was supposed to have left." Mrs. Terrizi's exact words had been "sneaking around like she was up to no good," but her son didn't consider this factual enough for a report, even an oral report. "And Mama says if she'd caught Mrs. Hampter in the kitchen again she'd remember all right because she'd have thrown the salad bowl at her. She says Mrs. Hampter went right down the hall after she was observed and out the front door."

"Was her car parked with the others out front?"

"Mama says she walked. And nobody we've talked to so far—except Mama—saw her after she left the terrace and went toward the greenhouse."

McDougal glanced at another report on the desk. "The Associated Press stringer got to the house at eight. He'd had an appointment with Dilman for Saturday morning, but Dilman called him back and changed it to that same evening." McDougal stopped, looked confused, and said, "I mean, last night, of course." *Last night* still sounded unreal to him, years removed from now. He thought of a line from some poem—was it Dylan Thomas?—Eileen had read aloud to him the first year they were married, something about "as far removed as a grief ago." He tried to shut out the sound of her voice and concentrate on what the sergeant was saying.

". . . made dinner even later, and Mama said Mrs. Dilman was sore as a wet hen about that. Doesn't make sense to have a reporter and a photographer running around when you've got guests ready to eat."

"From the scraps of conversation Lucy overheard, Dilman was using that as another stick to prod Mrs. Hampter: 'Either you apologize to Miss Coving now, and say you were wrong about the books, or I'll give the AP man a story that will . . .'" McDougal's voice trailed away.

The sergeant prompted him. "Kind of a threat to smear her, wasn't it? Can't you ask Mrs. Hampter right out, when you see her?"

The inspector shrugged. "Ask a direct question and you get a direct lie."

"But the homicide guy you were telling me about —the one you trained under—he said to start the questions soft and easy and then, when the suspect is off guard, wham in with the big one. . . ." But even as Terrizi said it, he was thinking, The inspector's in no shape to wham. Not with a dame like Georgina Hampter. Maybe if he gets some sleep . . . maybe tomorrow. . . . The sergeant couldn't think how to word this tactfully, and his misery showed on his open young face.

McDougal watched his protégé sardonically. Do

him good to learn it early on: never put your total faith in any one person or you'll crash like Humpty Dumpty. But another part of his mind rejected the cheap cynicism; he wanted to say something to make amends, to show he was still a responsible, functioning cop. But he sat frozen. I need a drink. I ought to knock off now and go buy a bottle. . . . First, whip up some job for Terrizi so he'll be off my neck—

The knock on the door exploded against his raw nerve ends like the crack of a rifle.

Terrizi leaped up to admit Sergeant Bayles. "Sir, Douglas Brill is here. He just left Dilman's widow, and he wants to know if he can see you right away."

With both young cops waiting expectantly, it was easier for McDougal to say yes than to invent plausible excuses.

All he could remember about Brill was that Brill had been one of the guests at the Dilmans' and Lucy had said, "Thank God that Doug was there. He was the only one I could really talk to all evening." And something about "used to take me to opening nights when Hal was away."

If, unconsciously, McDougal had formed an image of a suave New Yorker who knew the names of headwaiters and always had seats for opening nights, the man who came into Chief Salter's office was ludicrously wrong for the part: dumpy, with a huge head outlined in a frizz of gray hair, long dangling arms, and a glistening red face. "What the hell have you been doing, scaring two defenseless women?" He sounded hoarse and furious. "And what's all this about oleander? Barbara says you think she murdered Larry because she'd worked in a hospital and knew about the stuff."

Sereant Terrizi had relinquished his chair—it was

one of the two in Chief Salter's office; the inspector had the desk chair—and Brill collapsed into it.

"God, it's stifling in here. Mind if I take off my jacket?"

He was already extricating his long arms from the sleeves of a seersucker jacket; the inspector noted fastidiously that Brill's shirt was wet under the arms. For some reason this made him feel cooler, more collected. He said, "I'm sorry if Mrs. Dilman got that impression. We've been interviewing everybody who had dinner there—asking them all the same questions."

Sergeant Terrizi, who was standing against the wall, stirred—the smallest wriggle—but McDougal was conscious of it instantly and he took it as a protest and reproach; the sergeant had been in the greenhouse with him and had seen how he lost his temper with Dilman's widow.

"Sergeant, please take these reports to Bayles to be Xeroxed." He held out some papers.

Terrizi looked understandably confused. The police, to their bitter sorrow, didn't have their own Xerox copier; they had to use the one at the bank, and the bank was not open on Saturday. But the sergeant took the papers, did a turnabout that gave the impression of heel-clicking efficiency, and withdrew smartly.

Brill's face was still glistening, but he didn't look as angry now. "Joan Dilman was crying and carrying on, saying it was all her fault that you suspect her stepmother."

"We don't suspect anyone—yet."

"Barbara was crazy about that bastard. She coddled him like a baby after he had the coronary. And I doubt if she'd even have had time to get out to the greenhouse last night. She was running around looking for more briquets, and trying to keep Larry from getting too stoned, and going upstairs to comfort Joan, and coping with that fortissimo Italian cook. So she knows about oleander—so who doesn't? I've just come back from the Costa del Sol. Oleander all over the place."

"Did you know it was poisonous?"

Brill hesitated. "I remembered this afternoon when Barbara was telling me about the greenhouse. A waiter's kid at the government-run *parador* chewed on a stick of some bush and went into convulsions and died. Could have been oleander."

McDougal nodded. "Were you in the Dilmans' greenhouse yesterday?"

"Yes, as soon as I arrived. I stopped there first because I wanted to see if the gardener would do some work for me in his spare time. He wasn't there, so I went right along to the barbecue place and then to the terrace." He watched the inspector making notes. "And there's something I'd better tell you while we're at it: Dilman took my wife away twenty years ago, and I'd cheerfully have torn out his guts."

The inspector said, in a new, warm voice, "I don't blame you. . . . Cigarette?" He held out his package of Kents.

Brill shook his big head. "Emphysema." But he responded visibly to the change in atmosphere; he tilted his chair back and stretched his short legs to reach the floor. "I was a wreck for at least a year afterward. Every play I reviewed—or almost—I was in a mood to rip to shreds. I'd tear into the script or the acting or the direction or all three at once. It's a wonder Equity didn't go after my scalp and put it up on a pole outside some theater, as a warning."

McDougal was smiling; his long, bony face looked less gaunt.

"I even attacked Alison Moffat—but she's a good fighter. She saw me in the lounge of the Algonquin one night and came over and threw her drink in my face." He laughed. "So we've been friends ever after. But some of the other poor devils—I was frostbite when they were budding. I've often wondered when I read about some cop who worked over a suspect or got trigger-happy, doesn't that apply to your business too? A cop's marriage goes to hell so he takes it out on—"

"I'm not married," the inspector said curtly. He tried to draw on his cigarette, but his hand was trembling so badly he rammed the Kent into the ashtray instead. Brill was baiting him—as a theater man he would know all about Eileen and the director she'd married.

Brill seemed genuinely abashed. "I didn't mean anything personal. Just some of my meandering pseudopsychology. Drama critics are a bunch of pontificators. Anyway, I know you're the one who has Lucy's studio. She told me last night you were moving out, and I wanted her to rent it to me but she wouldn't. She'd been telling me she'll have to get a new tenant, but when it came right down to cases, she couldn't seem to face it. Sounds as if you're irreplaceable."

The sick, churning feeling in McDougal's middle subsided. He was touched by Lucy's loyalty, and he had an oddly magnanimous feeling for the man who'd tried to step into his place and been rebuffed. "Lucy thinks a lot of you. She told me how glad she was to see you at the Dilmans' last night."

Brill looked pleased. "We had a good talk. If it hadn't been for her—" His expression changed. "Say, Lucy's not the one who put the finger on Barbara . . . ?" The question mark hung in the air.

McDougal assured him that Lucy hadn't put the finger on Mrs. Dilman.

"Knowing Lucy, I'd have thought she'd pick Georgina Hampter as First Murderer."

The inspector kept a straight face.

"But Georgina had gone long before dinner."

"Do you remember exactly when she left the terrace and went to the greenhouse?"

"Just after eight. The AP man had already come for an interview, and Barbara sent me out to the driveway to keep them occupied—the photographer too—till Georgina was out of the way."

"So you didn't hear Mrs. Hampter apologize to Marcy Coving?"

"I caught the first part of it. Dilman was pulling the strings and feeding her the lines, and I'm automatically in sympathy with anybody Dilman gets his hooks into—even a stupid bitch like Hampter."

"You think he had some sort of hold on her?"

"I'm sure of it. But I can't figure out what. Hampter's a lunatic-fringe ranter, but she's never tried to hide it. And she's rich enough to get her own way, especially in a town like Wingate. But when she was gulping and groveling there on the terrace, she seemed kind of pathetic."

"Did you see her actually enter the greenhouse afterward?"

"Yes, it seems to me when I was coming across the lawn with the AP men. . . . I gather your theory is that she went in then and cut the substitute skewer. But how would she have made sure Larry got it?" He snapped his fingers. "Oh, the no-tomato, of course. Barbara had yapped that all over."

Either Douglas Brill was remarkably ingenuous or

he'd picked a profession on the wrong side of the footlights.

"But I can't remember her mentioning the no-tomato bit while Georgina was around."

"She repeated it to Mrs. Terrizi in the kitchen in front of Mrs. Hampter."

"Well, Georgina's a nasty piece of goods, and I suppose I should hope she's It. But if a playwright rigged his last act that way, I'd say, 'Totally unconvincing—out of character.'"

McDougal nodded involuntarily, then covered the slip by bending to scratch something on a memo pad.

"What does Georgina say about it?"

The inspector said they still hadn't interviewed her because she'd been at a meeting all afternoon.

"The thing is, I can't see her having the brains to figure out that bit with the skewer. Look at the bumbling way she went about getting those books out of the library; somebody was bound to figure out the kid hadn't acted on his own. But the trick with the oleander is different. With any luck, Larry's death would have passed for another heart attack. How did you get onto it?"

Scientific curiosity? McDougal wondered. He told Brill about the article he'd read on poisonous shrubs and plants in the *Times* garden section.

"Amazing memory you've got, Inspector. I'm glad I came clean with you right away. By the way, I hope I made it clear I did *not* harbor a murderous hatred for twenty years. I got my revenge watching Dilman and my ex-wife fight like a pair of gamecocks. But I knew how Solent felt last night when Dilman was starting the lover-boy pitch with the Coving girl. The girl wasn't having any at first, but after Georgina ate crow, Larry was the hero to kiss on both cheeks and

Solent was ready to knife him." Brill's fuzzy eyebrows wriggled. "H-m-m. From knifing to skewer gimmick— it's a logical jump. And Solent is bright enough to have thought of the oleander. I know it sounds crazy to want to kill somebody you've just met, but you didn't know Dilman. He affected people that way." Brill smiled wryly. "Primitive reaction. I've been there. But I'm certainly not claiming Solent's guilty. Just a guess out of left field."

"Alison Moffat says Solent was with her all the time during that last hour before dinner. She told Lucy this morning."

Brill's chair teetered suddenly; he braced his feet to steady it and lower the front legs to the floor. Then he fidgeted on the edge of the seat. "Look, if there isn't anything more right now—I asked Barbara and Joan to have early dinner with me, before we meet Barbara's sister at the airport; didn't think it was good for them to be alone in that house—and I have to pick up some food at Coleman's. Barbara didn't want to go to a restaurant; she's the what-would-people-think? type." He made a face. "As you may gather, she's not a close friend of mine, but she got a stinking deal from Larry last night, and she's in a bad state of nerves today. . . . I told her I'd see you and find out what I could. She'll feel better when I tell her you haven't singled her out to aim the noose at."

McDougal said, "I was too tough on her this morning, and I'm sorry." Hearing himself say it, he had a slight sense of release.

Brill sighed as he got up. "If there's anything I hate, it's having to do a Good Deed. Well, off to fix the funeral baked meats."

As the reluctant Samaritan went out the door, McDougal watched Brill's sagging, dumpy rear view

and straightened his own shoulders before looking at
his watch: 4:46. Time to see the Hampter woman on
the way home. And change his clothes before dinner.
. . . Lucy's guest. He was beginning to be curious about
Alison Moffat.

# 15

The guard on duty at the high school had a bogus Irish heartiness that always set Marcy Coving's teeth on edge. She knew vaguely he'd lost his right eye in an accident at some plant, and so she tried to overcompensate for her distaste of the man by smiling through his heavy-fisted gallantry, the how's-the-fair-colleen? approach. His one good eye protruded so eagerly when he stared at her it often seemed about to pop out and roll down inside her dress.

That Saturday afternoon she was braced for the usual weekend gambit in his limited repertoire—"Now, what's a pretty girl like you doing working on a fine day like this?"—but all she got was a sullen nod. No greeting, no would-be roguishness, no one-eyed going over. He was staring not at her but at the canvas book bag she was carrying, and for a weird moment she thought he was going to ask her to open it for inspection.

She was bringing back a half dozen plays Jeff Solent had taken out of the library earlier that week. He had brought the bag to Marcy's that noon, presumably so he could make notes over the weekend, and she had lugged them along this afternoon in a furious rush to remove all traces of a lover who had abandoned her just when she needed him most. Inspector McDougal's thunderbolt—Dilman was murdered—had left her shaky and bewildered. She had counted on being able to talk it all over with Jeff as soon as the inspector and the sergeant left them alone. Instead, Jeff had used her phone instantly—*her* phone —to make a lunch date with Alison Moffat. He had preferred to talk things over with that fat old woman just because she was famous—and maybe to revenge himself on Marcy for last night, which was incredibly unfair. It wasn't Lawrence Dilman's fame that had impressed her—certainly not. She, Marcy Coving, wasn't bedazzled like a teenybopper; she had merely been grateful to a charming, brilliant, older man, a distinguished author, who had made Georgina Hampter back down. After all, she had *not* gone to the greenhouse with Dilman. It was Jeff who'd gone to the greenhouse with that raddled old woman and had deliberately chosen to sit with Alison at dinner and laugh his fool head off at her stories. Oh, *he* had an alibi, all right.

And today he hadn't even stayed with Marcy long enough to comfort and reassure her. He had mumbled something about "See you later" and dashed off. If he thought he was going to use her apartment all weekend as a way station and study hall, he had another think coming. He'd find his books gone—and his girl.

The guard, Higgins (the students called him Higgy-Piggy), was taking so long to open the door of the library that Marcy let the book bag drop on the corridor floor with a thud. It may have been a symbolic gesture: drop Jeff.

"Going to be here awhile?" Higgins said.

Marcy said she didn't know. She had to keep herself from adding, And it's none of your business.

"You think you'll be here till five o'clock, say?"

"I told you, I have no idea. I have some work to do. . . ." Jeff would guess where she was; if he didn't come after her in an hour— "I'll put on the snap lock when I leave." She shut the door in Higgins's face but managed not to slam it.

As she went past the reading lounge into the big main room, she was irritably aware of the guard still standing in the corridor outside, watching.

Usually she had a special proprietary sense of pleasure if she came into the library when it was empty. Today, she felt so jangled that trivia attacked her like fleas: wilting forsythia in the vase on the circulation desk; one of the matted glossy photographs lurching crookedly on the far wall; a new scratch on a table. She put the book bag down on the desk, stuck her handbag in a drawer, and marched over to straighten the crooked photograph. Then she carried the vase of forsythia into the lavatory next to the equipment room and dumped out the water. Only one spray was hopelessly gone; she put that in a wastebasket, rearranged the others in fresh water, and put the vase back on the counter. By salvaging the bouquet, she had a faint, vicarious sense of reviving her wilted spirits.

As she emptied the book bag, she noted the titles of the plays mechanically, to check them in. But when she had all five spread out, the pattern suddenly leaped at her: *Ulysses in Nighttown* . . . *A Man for All Seasons* . . . *The Importance of Being Earnest* . . . *An Enemy of the People* . . . *Mahagonny.* Joyce's *Ulysses* banned; Thomas More beheaded; Wilde's work yanked out of libraries, banned from the stage, in the hysteria after his trial; Ibsen vilified; Brecht and Weill, Jews in Hitler's Germany. She was moved almost to tears. Jeff must have been planning a lecture on censorship, even after Con-Com's warning to play down "the book incident." As she looked at the books, the ripples of pride spread out and out, in her mind, till she felt they embraced oceans and continents and centuries. In art, she thought, it's not the survival of the fittest, because each generation has its own standards of what's fit. She remembered an ex-English Lit teacher she'd met in library school. The woman had told her emotionally, "They wanted me to teach a course in the Modern Novel—to relate to the present. I'd have had to stand up there and talk to the students as if I considered this dreadful modern stuff literature. And I couldn't do it, I simply couldn't. So I'm going to be a librarian."

The logic, or illogic, of it had fascinated Marcy. "But those same books will be in a library."

And the woman had said on a note of triumph, "All I'll have to do is check them in and out. I won't have to read them or talk about them."

Marcy wondered again now what sort of librarian the woman would make. Maybe she'll put gold stars on the books she approves of and a skull and crossbones on the baddies. Or maybe she'll just conveniently lose the one she detests. Or break their spines and keep them in limbo forever—Withdrawn for Repair.

Ibsen's spine was coming loose; it needed to be sent out for rebinding, but Marcy had a tender protective instinct to keep it at home during the current crisis. She took it into her small office, got out a roll of stitched linen tape, and mended the center fold. The roll was almost finished, and she made a note on a memo pad: *Add to Gaylord order—3 Linen Tape, No. 37.*

One section of her shelf-list inventory record was on the desk, with a marker inserted at S. She had been working on the inventory since mid-April, mostly during study periods or first thing in the mornings, and now she decided rather drearily to get on with the job.

But as she walked through the fiction stacks carrying her shelf list and began checking S, the feeling of drudgery evaporated. Salinger: *Catcher in the Rye* had been cited in ALA bulletins as the book most frequently banned in school libraries, and Marcy had a buoying sense of victory because Georgina Hampter had missed it. . . . Scott: She smiled on Sir Walter with affection, as one smiles on a sweet old grandfather. . . . Sholokhov: No Red Menace scare right now. . . . Steinbeck: Five Steinbecks still on the shelf. As she checked them on her list, she said silently, I'll get your *Grapes of Wrath* back, I promise. . . . Swift, Jonathan: *Gulliver* had survived. . . . She began to feel peaceful and happy, in this world without boundaries.

She had got as far as Twain when a loud voice shattered the stillness. "Miss Coving! Where are you, Miss Coving?"

Con-Com. What was the superintendent of schools doing here on a Saturday afternoon? Jeff had once described him as a "devout pillar of the Wingate Christian Country Club."

"I'm in the stacks, Mr. Bolling." Perversely, she stood there listening, like a game of hide-and-seek, while the footsteps clopped through the stacks. Has his golf shoes on.

"Miss Coving!" Even his pinkish bald spot looked agitated.

She saw the trademark lizard on the pocket of his mesh golf shirt; chameleon, she thought, as he adapted his face to the cautiously genial let's-talk-this-over expression.

He seemed to be having trouble getting started. "If we could go into your office—er, one or two things—"

As he sat in the chair beside her desk, facing the window, she noted with detachment that the pores in his nose looked like moon craters. He put a car key down on the desk and twiddled it absently. The gesture reminded her of something—something to do with Jeff—and without knowing why, she began to feel uneasy.

"I realize Lawrence Dilman's death must have upset you, and I'm sure that's why you reacted so impulsively, coming here today."

She was puzzled. "It's not impulsive to finish my inventory."

"Inventory? But I understood you brought in a satchel of books to replace the ones that were—er—removed."

"Who told you that?" She was too angry to bother straightening him out.

"Higgins called Mrs. Hampter, and she—uh—got in touch with me."

"Is the guard a spy for Mrs. Hampter?"

"Certainly not. That's a most unfair accusation, Miss Coving. She got Higgins this job after he was injured in her husband's plant, and out of loyalty—you know how these old fellows are—he feels responsible to the school."

"He feels responsible to Mrs. Hampter. I'm the one who feels responsible to the students."

"I hoped I'd made it clear the other day that for the best interests of the school we must avoid doing anything drastic right now."

He was diddling with the car key again, and the formless worry about Jeff surged back and distracted her from listening.

". . . grant you the books were removed in a somewhat high-handed manner, but I've had dozens of phone calls from parents who think Mrs. Hampter was right."

She said suddenly, "The world is round."

Con-Com looked astonished. "Nobody questions that."

"But once students weren't allowed to learn it. They had to believe the world was flat because their parents thought so, and that's how it had to be. And now, if we let them see only the pretty side of life—"

"Unformed young minds can't digest too much violence and biased propaganda."

"These kids were weaned on violence. Do you think all they watch is *Sesame Street* and *Lassie?* As for propaganda, just let them listen to a campaign speech or any TV commercial. And protecting them from four-letter words! If their parents saw the stuff scrawled on the walls in the rest rooms—"

Unexpectedly, Con-Com grinned. "At least they can't ask us to burn down the rest rooms. Cost too much money to replace." The grin became pained. "I don't like book burning any more than you do, Miss Coving. But I'm sure we can work out a compromise so everybody's happy. All I ask is that you wait till after the meeting Monday night before you do anything. We'll hear all sides and—"

"And get caught in the middle."

"I'll admit there are considerable pressures."

He looked so worried and perspiring she felt rather sorry for him. "I wasn't replacing the books today anyway." She explained about Jeff's leaving the plays in her apartment.

Bolling looked even more worried. He diddled again with the car key, and Marcy felt the same frantic need to pinpoint whatever it reminded her of.

"I feel reluctant to mention this, but there have been—er—rather strongly worded complaints about your—uh—friendship with Mr. Solent."

It seemed so silly and unimportant, compared to her undefined fear, that she came near smiling.

"I know that in this day and age your private affairs should be your own business. After all, if college students can shack up in a dorm . . . but—uh—in a community of this sort—"

"Would you like me to resign?"

Con-Com seemed shocked by so direct a question. "All I meant was, a word to the wise—"

"You mean we should sneak off to a motel in another county whenever we want to make love?"

"Well—er—I wouldn't go so far as to . . ." He squirmed off the hook. "Say, I have one piece of good news I should have told you right away. Mrs. Hampter said that in view of Lawrence Dilman's untimely death—"

"You mean his untimely murder."

"Miss Coving, it would be irresponsible of us to repeat an unfounded rumor. I heard some gossip at the club, but—"

"Inspector McDougal doesn't gossip."

She didn't hear what Con-Com said next. She only saw what he did with his right hand; he reached out for the car key and put it back in his pants pocket. She had a blinding flashback: Jeff putting something out on the table in her apartment, fiddling with it while she talked, then palming it as soon as the inspector said, *Alison Moffat has given you an alibi.*

# 16

Tipped off by Sergeant Bayles's girl, Zora, the inspector turned down his hostess's offer of liquid refreshment. Even if it had been a bona fide, 86-proof offer, he no longer felt the urge to grab at the genie in a bottle, on duty or off. The wrenching pain he'd lived with for twenty-four hours was quieter now than it had been all day. He was sitting on a brown velvet sofa that looked like plush horsehair, and he was concentrating on Georgina Hampter so totally there wasn't room for anything else in the front of his mind. What interested him most was that this rigidly handsome, aggressive woman seemed offhand when he asked her how long she'd been in the greenhouse.

"Probably two or three minutes. What on earth does it matter?"

She worked up to what struck him as a genuine air of grievance.

"I must say, if the police in this town spend their time asking silly questions of honest citizens instead of going after the dope addicts and peddlers of pornography . . ."

The p's in "peddlers" and "pornography" fairly popped out of her mouth.

It reminded McDougal of his talk with Chief Salter, who had returned to headquarters just before he left and had been visibly shaken at the thought of the inspector's having to tackle Georgina Hampter. "Better you than me. You know what she wanted me to do yesterday? She came in here practically waving a spear and ordered me to go over to the newsstand and confiscate every magazine with a nude centerfold. She told me, 'Once you have removed the centerfold, you may put the magazines back in the rack.' What's she expect me to do with the nudes—put 'em up for *Most Wanted* posters?"

Georgina Hampter didn't berate the inspector about nude centerfolds, but she did announce as soon as he arrived that she had paid for every book she destroyed, so the police had no right to hound her.

McDougal assured her he hadn't come to discuss the book burning. "Words would fail me," he said drily. "We are simply asking some routine questions of all the people who were at the Dilmans' last evening." Watching her subside, he was amused, as often before, that the phrase "routine questions" had so calming an effect. It was lucky the interviewees didn't know that 90 percent of police cases were solved by police asking "routine questions."

Georgina not only showed no hesitation in saying yes when he asked her if she'd been in the greenhouse, she also admitted readily that she'd gone back to the kitchen. "I saw that fat old woman in the weird outfit coming down the walk to the greenhouse and I wanted to avoid her, so I went through the passageway to the kitchen and left by the kitchen door."

"Mrs. Terrizi says she saw you afterward in the back hall."

For the first time, she was frightened and made a desperate effort not to show it. "If you must know, I was going to the Little Girls' Room."

Ordinarily, the idiotic euphemism would have made McDougal scowl, but all he said now was, "Oh, of course, you'd been in Dilman's office with him earlier, so you knew where it was."

"Mr. Dilman wanted to talk to me about those books in private"—she was talking too fast—"*Wayward the World* and the others, so he took me into his office."

"And that's when he persuaded you to change your mind and admit to Miss Coving you'd been wrong?"

Even the reminder of that humiliating scene on the terrace made her angry enough to fight back. "I was right all along."

"Then what pressure did Dilman use to make you reverse yourself?"

Her pale blue eyes flickered. "He appealed to my sympathy. He was a very sick man—his heart. I gave in because I felt sorry for him. But when I got home and thought it over, I realized I couldn't back down. I'd have been letting down all the decent-minded people in this town."

"And Dilman is no longer around to persuade you." The inspector's ironic tone put "persuade" in heavy black quotation marks. "His death came at a very convenient time for you."

She said rather grandly, "We cannot question God's will."

"A lot of dubious things have been credited to God's will. But not murder."

"He wasn't murdered. He had a coronary. The hospital said so."

"He was poisoned. The autopsy proves it was murder."

She sat very still. Finally, in almost a whisper, she said, "Then the police—they'll be at the Dilman house. They'll be all over the place."

It was the oddest reaction he'd ever run into, from a suspect. He wished Lucy could have heard it.

Lucy didn't give him a chance to get beyond the preliminary facts: the hacked oleander, the hidden knife with traces of poison, and the later autopsy findings not just on Dilman but on the dog. She then leaped headfirst into an account of her own discovery at the Thrift Shop.

". . . So obviously Larry and Georgina had an affair way back when they were both on that Wingate Two Hundred committee, and he used that as blackmail so she killed him."

Lucy had forgotten her plan to let McDougal think he'd figured out the solution himself. Anyway, she had used up all her patience in the hour before he appeared. She had come home overflowing with news, to find the guest room door closed and a notice pinned on; it was written on the back side of a sheet torn from a desk calendar. *Need a nap—call me at six thirty.*

Insultingly terse. As if Lucy were a hotel desk clerk. She vented her annoyance in the bathroom by making as much noise as possible: yanking the shower curtains back and forth till the curtain rings rattled like castanets, dropping the bath brush, slamming the door of the medicine chest when she got out her eye drops. The answering silence roared in her head.

It was still roaring, or buzzing angrily, when she looked out the kitchen window and saw McDougal's car in front of the studio. By the time he came to the house, twenty minutes later, she was so impatient she couldn't bother building up his ego. It was her own ego that needed feeding. She wanted to be told what a clever detective she'd been, to find the real motive for the killing. As soon as she finished her dramatic account, she sat back, as if on the peak of a climax, to wait for applause.

McDougal sat on his hands. "I still can't see Georgina Hampter as a killer."

It was too maddening. "You couldn't see a black widow spider on the end of your nose."

"Probably not."

She noticed, belatedly, that he'd put on his new gray and white checked sports jacket, in honor of her guest, and that he looked desperately tired. Her better instincts swarmed to the rescue. "We both need a drink. Did you get any lunch?"

McDougal, recognizing a truce when he heard one, had the sense to accept the role of male-to-be-clucked-over. For once, he rather welcomed it. "Terrizi and I went to the Hungry Bear, but I didn't feel much like eating."

"No wonder. The din in that place is hideous. We'll have a quiche with our drinks. Only takes a minute to heat. I'm famished myself. Alison went rushing off to lunch with Jeff Solent...."

Along with a plate of hot quiche, Lucy gave the inspector a lively account of the Evans child carrying her petition to the Hungry Bear while the Thrift Shop turned up a prom dress. "I owed her a dress because she's the one who told me her mother had been on a committee with Larry and Georgina. And when I heard that, I went right to work on Liz Carmody."

This time, after quiche and two ounces of Scotch, McDougal was more receptive. "I think you've dug up the reason for the blackmail, all right. Dilman could have used the Associated Press man as a phony threat to make her come around faster—'Either you apologize to Miss Coving or I'll drop a few hints.' Not that the AP would give a damn about a silly affair that's ancient history."

"Georgina wouldn't realize that. To her, it was the Great Guilty Secret. And after all, she's set herself up as the Goddess of Purity, yelling about not corrupting our youth. That was Larry's pitch when I was in the phone alcove and heard them. He told her, 'I'm sure the reporter would be fascinated with any tidbits about that pillar of rectitude, Georgina Hampter.' Liz said he used to call her Georgie Porgie, and he called her that last night when he was twisting her arm to make her go out on the terrace and crawl."

"But it would have been Dilman's word against hers. She could have denied everything."

"Not if he had proof. If she'd written him some wild love letters he could show the AP man."

The inspector marveled at women's ignorance of the law. "No newspaper would touch them."

"Oh, nonsense. Newspapers love scattering dirt."

McDougal raised his voice. "It's illegal to print anybody's letters without permission. They'd be sued."

"Well, they *should* be sued," Lucy said. "I certainly wouldn't have wanted my love letters spread around."

The inspector, watching her, felt a tweak of jealousy. She had never written him anything more torrid than *Beef stew on stove on Sim.* But she was the kind of woman who would have let herself go—gloriously. In contrast . . . He said, "I can't imagine Georgina Hampter ever writing a love letter."

"That's what I would have said about—" She stopped just in time, teetering on the verge of "Alison," then grabbed for a substitute: "About a lot of people who seem in full control of their lives. But they can go clear off the track when it comes to loving some stinker. You ought to know."

When she saw his face tighten, she realized how it had sounded.

"I mean, you homicide men see that sort of thing all the time. And Larry Dilman had that effect on women." She went on quickly. "Did you see Barbara and Joan? How are they? That's a stupid question. They must be devastated. I should have gone over there today, but you made me feel so muzzled. I'd have felt like a hypocrite, going along with the heart attack story." In an endearing burst of honesty, she said, "The real reason I didn't was that I was just plain selfish. I wanted to go to the Thrift Shop because detecting is so much more fun than going to see a new widow I don't much like anyway. Did you give Barbara any notion it was murder?"

"She caught us hacking up a chair in the greenhouse, so I couldn't exactly say we'd come to offer our condolences." He described what had happened, with certain omissions, most notably his savage spurt of temper against the widow. "Joan says Barbara insisted on shish kebab for sinister reasons, but she recanted later. It seems to be the classic hate-stepmother twist."

"Whoever wrote Cinderella has a lot to answer for. Poor Barbara—she couldn't be really wicked. She's too damn boring and wholesome."

"She knew oleander was poisonous. They had a case of it when she worked in a hospital in Florida. We're lousy with suspects who know oleander—in Florida, Vietnam, Spain, California—"

"Oh, God, I forgot to call Alison."

An hour later, Lucy was wishing sourly that she'd forgotten to call Alison till the next morning. Her houseguest, resplendent again in the caftan and clanking bracelet, had taken over McDougal and even made him laugh out loud, which was really going too far. Lucy, stuck in the kitchen, was cross that she'd planned a hollandaise sauce she couldn't turn her back on. Through the open door to the living room, she could hear most of Alison's performance.

It had started off as an interview. Yes, indeed, Alison said, she and her husband had known Dilman when they all lived in the Village. In no time she'd veered into a rollicking account of how Larry had dangled his baby out the window on a rope. "Once a passerby called the fire department to rescue the child, and the fire trucks came roaring down Perry Street and they set up a ladder to grab the baby from the dog basket, and next we heard Larry shouting, 'Do you have to make so much noise? I'm working.'"

That was when McDougal laughed out loud, or at least made the involuntary half snort indicating (with him) uncontrollable merriment.

He'd better stop being so damn amused and get down to business, Lucy thought. She pressed freshly ground pepper into the steak, turned on the oven to Broil, and slammed in the broiler pan.

". . . always monstrously single-minded," Alison was saying. "But when he got his own way, he could be delightful. And of course, being in the theater I could make allowances for the prima donna streak in him. His first two wives were too young and naïve to understand that. But when he eloped with Doug Brill's wife—Madeline Brill, the actress—" Pause, gasp. "Oh, I hope I haven't given away any secrets. Doug is an old and dear friend."

Lucy fumed. Why, you bitch! You deliberately tossed in a motive for Doug. She stirred the hollandaise as if it were a witches' cauldron.

The inspector said, "You mustn't feel you're betraying a friend. Mr. Brill told me the story today. In fact, he said he understood how Jeff Solent might want to murder Dilman even on first acquaintance."

"What a fantastic idea. Drama critics always want to tie up loose ends into sinister knots."

"Then you don't think young Solent was violently angry at Dilman?"

"Oh, he snapped and snarled like a puppy but he forgot about it five minutes later. He's a remarkably well-adjusted young man, Inspector. And he certainly didn't diddle around with oleander. I was with him in the greenhouse, and I can vouch for that."

"Georgina Hampter mentioned seeing you come down the walk to the greenhouse—alone."

"Jeff was right behind me." Delicious, rueful laugh. "Look at me, Inspector. Can you imagine anybody being able to walk *abreast* of me, on a narrow walk? I'm sure Jeff confirmed my account."

"He would have told you that at lunch."

The throaty laugh again, but just a shade off. "I'm embarrassed to admit it, but at lunch we were talking about my old movies. At my age—old and forgotten—to find you're admired by somebody young is incredibly satisfying. That blessed sound of applause; without it we're dead. I always thought Peter Pan's Tinker Bell was ridiculous, but the older I get the more I realize that somebody has to clap or we're finished."

Even Lucy was moved. But she objected to the inspector being so moved himself. He sounded downright fatuous, saying Alison's fans must come in all ages, shapes, and sizes. "Solent and Douglas Brill are two of your greatest admirers."

Alison made modest, deprecating noises. "So generous. . . . And of course I didn't mean that Doug Brill could have nursed a viper of revenge in his bosom—do men have bosoms? Those who have shouldn't— Anyway, I'm sure Doug got over his murderous rage years ago."

"He's still a suspect with a good motive."

Lucy came to the doorway brandishing a carving knife. "Doug is *not* a suspect. He was with me every minute."

"How fortunate we all moved around two by two," Alison cooed. "All except the Hampter woman."

"I'm still not—"

A timer squawked on the stove. Lucy raced back to silence it and pour the brandy over the steak before she dumped the asparagus into the colander.

She was so impatient to serve dinner and become an active participant in the talk that she bustled her guests to the dinner table as bossily as a nanny, cutting them off in mid-sentence.

The steak à poivre was superb, but the hostess had to point this out herself. She and McDougal did the real eating. Alison fiddled with her food—it might have been plastic props on a dinner table in a stage set—and talked while the others chewed.

193

"I'm fascinated by your analysis of Georgina Hampter," she said to the inspector. "That she's a bigot and a bully but doesn't have the brains to plot a subtle way to get rid of Larry."

Before Lucy could swallow a mouthful of fresh asparagus and interrupt, Alison swept on.

"My theory is that Larry was the only one of us capable of murder."

"Except that somebody killed him first," Lucy said. "And Georgina had even more of a motive than you know." She began to tell about her detecting at the Thrift Shop that afternoon. In her hurry to take over, she said unthinkingly, "It was exactly like Larry to have to make a conquest of a big, bossy woman, just to amuse himself." When she saw Alison's eyes blaze, she realized what she'd done, and tried to atone. "It's not as if Georgina was talented or witty or well known." Not the same as his making love to you, she was trying to say.

The inspector seemed not to notice the interplay. He said to Alison, "You mean what you call Larry's 'monstrous single-mindedness' made him capable of murder? That interests me."

Alison's beaky nose quivered like a hound's on the scent. "He was not only capable, he planned the whole thing. He meant to murder Barbara."

"But she wasn't the one who was to have the shish kebab without tomato."

"That's what was so clever of him. At the last minute, just as dinner was served, Larry meant to raise hell about not having tomato on his. And Barbara would have given him her plate just to shut him up—nursie humoring patient. But I think Larry got so drunk he forgot to switch. So he murdered himself."

194

Lucy said, "If you want to play Sherlock Holmes, you ought to change costumes." She fixed an unfriendly look on her guest's charm bracelet. "You couldn't even figure out this morning where you lost your damn dingle-dangle. Some detective."

"Oh, I found it under my bedside table." Alison fingered the gold clown with the ruby nose. "See."

"That's not the one you lost. You had the clown this morning." Lucy squinted her eyes nearly shut, trying to remember, and her artist's memory offered up a picture as detailed as a color slide. "It was the bird in the cage; that's what was missing."

"Lucy is always so positive. The wronger she is, the more positive." Alison held up her wrist to point out the tiny caged bird on the bracelet. "I've had it right along."

The inspector acted like a small boy who's caught sight of a new gadget. "Might I see it?"

Lucy gave him a what-the-hell's-come-over-you? look, but Alison undid the clasp and handed the bracelet over.

While McDougal fingered the various trinkets, Alison kept up a chatty commentary. ". . . Bought the clown on the Rue Vendôme just after we saw the Frattelini Brothers, the great clowns of the Medrano. . . . That little crystal oblong with the gold handles was from Von Stellheim, the Hollywood director. He was old and ill, and he decided he wasn't going to be cheated out of the fun of his own funeral. So he had a glass coffin put in his drawing room in Beverly Hills and invited friends to a party. When we got there, he was sitting in the coffin majestically, receiving his guests and tossing out flowers. These tiny coffins were party favors for the women."

"And this bird?"

"Nothing much. A bauble from Japan." She reached out for the bracelet, but McDougal seemed not to notice. He was poking the delicate cage with his forefinger. "A remarkable piece of workmanship."

Alison was so quiet that Lucy felt called on to make small talk. "Alison was telling me last night that when she toured Japan she was intrigued with the way they keep larks in cages like canaries, so a Jap movie mogul had this made for her. If you shake it a certain way, it tweets in high C."

The inspector seemed even more fascinated. "Mind if I try it?" He didn't wait for permission; he jiggled the cage till the bird performed and then listened to the tinkled *tweet-tweet* as if it were Mozart.

Lucy felt edgy, and now it wasn't the social uneasiness of a hostess but a tension that pulled her nerve ends. "Mac, stop playing with that twittery thing and pour us more wine."

He had just got up to fetch the bottle from a side table when the phone rang.

"Get it, will you? If it's Liz Carmody, tell her I'll call her back after dinner."

The two women sat in that suspended animation of people who do and don't want to listen to somebody else's conversation. They couldn't actually hear what McDougal was saying on the hall phone, but as Lucy remarked after several minutes, "It's sure as hell not Liz Carmody. Probably the pathologist calling from the lab, to recite the latest ghoulish findings."

"In Japan," Alison said oddly, "they also roast larks and sell them on stands like roast chestnuts."

"That's all I need to hear. And as for your asinine theory that Larry meant to kill Barbara—" She broke off as McDougal came back into the room. "If it's ghoulish, don't tell us." Then she saw his tightened face and said fearfully, "Is somebody else dead?"

"Joan Dilman's in the hospital. Concussion. When it started to rain she went back to the house to close the windows, and somebody bashed her over the head."

# 17

The young state cop who had been on guard duty at the Dilman house was over six feet, as tall as Inspector McDougal, but at the moment he was hunched with anxiety. "I asked to see her driver's license, sir, just to make sure it was Miss Dilman. And she had her house key, so I let her go in alone. I guess I should have gone in with her. Is she—is she badly hurt?"

"The concussion's not too severe," McDougal said. "I just came from the hospital. The doctor thinks she'll be conscious by tomorrow."

The boy took a deep breath and stretched to his normal height.

"And it wasn't your fault, it was mine. I should have assigned at least two men to the place. You couldn't be expected to cover the front and rear and the greenhouse."

"No other car came in, sir. I'd swear to that."

The inspector nodded. "They're checking the back path now, for footprints. And we got a good clear cast of the prints under this window."

They were in Dilman's office, where a fingerprint man was already dusting the windowsill. In the sporadic glare of a police photographer's strobe lights, the gold lettering on the leather-bound books blinked on again, off again—Lawrence Dilman . . . Lawrence Dilman . . . Lawrence Dilman—like a miniature neon sign.

"I found her right there by the door." The young cop was oblivious to anybody but McDougal. "She'd said she'd only be a minute, but I figured with women that can mean anything up to twenty–thirty minutes so I didn't get worried at first. I stayed right out front near her car, so's I'd be sure to see her when she left. Then I heard a phone ringing and ringing, so I came in and saw her on the floor and I—I thought she was dead. When I got a pulse"—he smiled all over his nice young face—"it was like I'd been given a million dollars."

The inspector said with unusual warmth, "I felt that way myself when the doctor told me she'd be OK."

All the way to the hospital, he had blamed himself bitterly for his carelessness; his torments over his ex-wife seemed suddenly a miserably inadequate excuse. The fierce self-blame intensified when he saw Joan Dilman lying unconscious on the hospital bed, her face as white as her bandaged head. She looked much younger, and appallingly defenseless, her arm rigged to the contraption dripping glucose into her veins. "Still in shock," the doctor muttered. "If she hadn't been brought in right away, we'd be in real trouble." When he gave McDougal the cheering news from the skull X-rays, the inspector had felt such a surge of thankfulness it was like a reprieve.

He said to the young state cop now, "Your finding her within minutes of the attack was what really saved her." If it was an overstatement, this seemed the time for overstatements. "Stop worrying. She'll definitely be all right."

As soon as the boy had left, McDougal decided to call Lucy to give her the same reassuring news. A fingerprint man was working at the desk where the phone was, so the inspector went out to the extension in the hall alcove.

Sitting down to dial, he jackknifed his long legs under the shelf and saw the uphill scrawl on the memo pad—unmistakably Lucy's handwriting—*Plaza Hotel, PL 9-3000*. She had tried to reach him—when? She hadn't mentioned it today, so she hadn't been calling him officially, to report trouble. It must have been soon after she got here last evening. How the hell had she known he wouldn't be at the airport? Terrizi? But the sergeant hadn't arrived till after she left, when Dilman was in the ambulance. Mrs. Terrizi! Mama must have picked up some worry signals from her son, and what Mrs. Terrizi took in, she instantly gave out, amplified a hundredfold. And Lucy had been concerned enough to leave her old friend Doug Brill and her host and the others and rush to a phone. The chain of concern for him—from sergeant to mama to Lucy—made him feel unexpectedly gratified.

Lucy answered on the first ring and, when he reported on Joan, said, "Thank God. I've been sitting here calling myself horrible names because I stayed away from Joan and Barbara all day."

McDougal said, "If I'd listened to you about Georgina, I'd have had the house well enough covered so that nobody could have sneaked in."

Lucy showed unusual restraint in skipping the I-told-you-so's. "You must be exhausted. It's almost midnight. Can't somebody else take over?"

"I'm not tired." Surprisingly, it was true. His voice sounded strong and re-crisped. "As soon as the fingerprint men finish in the office I want to make a real search for the letters, but I'm afraid they're already gone."

"Look in the middle desk drawer first. It was partly open when Alison and I were in Larry's office before dinner."

Miraculously, the letters were still there, nine of them, not tied up in a packet but rammed into a manila envelope marked G. The inspector opened one and began to read, to make certain, but it was so nakedly revealing he soon skipped down to the signature—*Your own Georgie Porgie*—with a row of X's for kisses.

Terrizi came in while McDougal was staring at the X's. The inspector glanced up, saw a smear of lipstick on the sergeant's left cheek, just northwest of the mouth, and said, "I'm sorry to have interrupted your evening with Angie."

Terrizi grabbed for his handkerchief and rubbed frantically.

"Other side. If you want a mirror, the bathroom's right in there." He pitched his voice mercifully low, so the other men wouldn't hear.

The sergeant came back looking scrubbed almost raw in one spot. "I came as fast as I could, but it took them a while to locate me." He didn't feel called on to add that he'd been located on an obscure back road known locally as Honeysuckle Lane. "What happened?"

McDougal told him. "And after the way I bungled things, I'm luckier than I deserve." He showed Terrizi the pile of letters. "I think Dilman went up to his old office over the garage and dug them out Friday afternoon. His wife said he insisted on going up there, although he wasn't supposed to climb stairs. And of course he showed the letters to Georgina so she'd knuckle under. My guess is, she came back from the greenhouse later to try to get them while everybody else was on the terrace or wherever, but she ran into your mother in the hall and couldn't risk it then. So she tried again tonight—and panicked when Joan came in. Grabbed up a vase and bashed Joan, then got out through the window before the state cop came back. She got in that way, too."

"It's kind of an amateur operation." Terrizi was examining the window screen. "Looks as if she ripped it open with nail scissors or something. What would she have done if the window was already closed and locked?"

"Smashed it in. We found a rock right under the window. They're testing for prints."

"All amateurs wear gloves," one of the fingerprint men said. He was spraying powder on the doorjamb. "Even ten-year-old vandals. I think we're getting a few partials here and there, but they may be Dilman's."

The photographer said cheerily, "You know what I read somewhere? If you're eating human flesh, the palm of the hand is the tastiest, and fingers are sort of like spareribs."

"If inflation keeps up, that may be a very useful tip. How about feet? Filet of sole?"

The inspector said, "I'll eat somebody's old sole if the cast of that footprint doesn't turn out to match Hampter's."

"You think she killed Dilman?" the sergeant said.

"I think we'll go see her right now." McDougal picked up the letters.

Almost as soon as they were in the car, the police radio jabbered with news of the plaster cast: size nine sneaker, C width.

"Sounds pretty big for a woman," Terrizi said. "How about Douglas Brill and Jeff Solent?"

"Brill and Mrs. Dilman were together at his house. He was giving the women dinner before he drove to the airport to pick up Mrs. Dilman's sister. When Joan didn't come right back after she went to close the windows during the rain, they were worried and called the house and couldn't get an answer. They got here just after the cop found Joan unconscious."

"And Solent?"

"They aren't *his* love letters. And he has unusually long narrow feet. Didn't you notice this noon?"

Terrizi shook his head dejectedly.

"You noticed something a damn sight more important. If it hadn't been for you, I wouldn't have connected what happened later. . . ." He elaborated on this for several minutes. The sergeant stopped looking dejected. The speedometer, zooming to an illegal seventy, reflected his elation.

He had just stopped the car in front of the Hampter house when the inspector said, "The sneakers. She wouldn't track mud inside."

"Not if my mama saw her," Terrizi said. "I have to leave my shoes outside like the house was a sacred temple. I'll look around out back."

"That garage connects with the house—probably a door into a side hall. When she put the car away, she might have left the sneakers there. My hunch is she wouldn't have the wits to hide them. Take a look, and I'll go on in."

He had to push the bell for several minutes before Georgina Hampter came to the door in a tailored robe and an aura of indignation. "This is an outrage. I was already asleep. I refuse to see anyone at this hour."

203

The inspector held out one of the letters. "This is yours, I believe."

Her right hand reached out involuntarily, then jerked back. "I don't know what you're talking about."

"We found your fingerprints on the windowsill of Dilman's office."

"You couldn't have. I wore—" She stopped so abruptly that the *wore* was half swallowed.

"Yes, and you wore size nine sneakers, C width. We got a perfect print."

As if on cue, Terrizi came out of the garage dangling the muddy sneakers tied together by the laces. "There's mud in her car, too."

Georgina said hoarsely, "You have no right. It's unconstitutional to invade private property and—"

"Coming from you, that's an especially interesting statement. Either you talk here or you'll come with us to headquarters. Of course you're entitled to call your lawyer."

"He was my husband's lawyer. I don't want him to know. . . . I'll talk to you in private, but not—" She pointed to Sergeant Terrizi.

For the inspector, the next ten minutes seemed endless. Georgina, sitting in the same chair she'd sat in on his earlier visit, was a travesty of that woman, babbling on and on. "I didn't dare be seen there, and when I heard somebody coming I grabbed the nearest thing and swung. It sounded so loud, like splitting a coconut. Then the phone rang and rang. I heard the cop coming before I could get the letters. If you let me have them and don't tell anybody, I'll never cause any more trouble. I'll call off the meeting Monday. I won't get the librarian fired on a morals charge. . . ." It would have been ludicrous if it hadn't been sickening. "Larry put me through hell. He said if I didn't do what he told me to, he'd show the letters to the AP man. He said the story would get around and I'd be the laughingstock of Wingate. If you'll give me the letters, I'll let that girl replace the books. . . ."

McDougal's voice cut like an ice-cold knife through the hysterical babbling. "The police have no intention of using your letters to shut you up. I despise your brand of censorship, but blackmail is even worse. The letters won't be made public unless it's necessary to use them for evidence at the trial."

"I didn't kill Larry! I didn't."

"I haven't said you did. You'll be charged with breaking and entering, assault and battery. I'd advise you to get a lawyer immediately."

"Chief Salter wouldn't put me in jail." She was beginning to sound like the old Georgina. "And I have to chair the meeting Monday night."

Terrizi said, "With her, bail money's no problem. But if I'd been in her shoes, you know how I'd have got rid of those sneakers? I'd have tossed 'em on the town dump. By the time we thought of looking there—
pfui—nothing left but ashes."

"You're developing the criminal mind," the inspector said. "In a cop, that's a pearl without price—provided you don't have a price. Keep your eyes on the road; I wasn't impugning your virtue. Now all you have to do is think like the murderer. My theory is that it wasn't meant to work out the way it did. . . ."

He talked till they got to the studio. Then he yawned so broadly his jawbone creaked.

"See you in the morning. And, sergeant, tell Angie I couldn't have managed without you. And I like the color of her lipstick."

He lay on the single bed and looked at the

phone. Take the receiver off the hook, so that if Eileen tries to reach me again . . .

You're on a case, he told himself harshly, and switched off the light.

Twice during the night he was yanked from sleep, thinking he heard the phone. Both times, he lifted the receiver—and got a dial tone.

# 18

"And don't try to distract me with sex." Marcy was slightly disheveled but fully clothed and vibrating with righteousness. "I asked you a serious question and I want a serious answer."

"Is that how you think of sex," Jeff Solent said, "as a distraction? Then you'll never be a fit wife and mother. I'm glad I found out in time."

"Answer me." She sounded rather clenched-lip.

"All right, so I was alone for a while in the greenhouse. Are you implying I murdered that bastard?"

"Don't you call him that."

"Why? He was a bastard alive. Now he's a dead bastard. And he's even more trouble dead than alive. Stick to the point. Do you think I killed him?"

"N-n-no. I don't know what to think. All I know is you lied to the inspector and—"

"I did not lie to the inspector."

"But if you were alone in the greenhouse, you should have said so. Why did you let Alison Moffat cover up for you?"

He said wearily, "I didn't know she was going to."

"And then instead of talking it over with me, you rush off to her."

"For a bloody good reason—which I can't go into now."

"That's what I mean. You won't *tell* me. And you put something on the table and played with it—and then you hid it from the inspector as soon as he talked about alibis. Was it a key?"

"A key!" He laughed oddly. "You might call it that."

"I'm fed to the teeth with your double-talk."

"And I'm fed to the teeth with you bugging me. I came here because I'm in trouble, and I counted on you to show you love me—period. And what do I get? You push me away and squeal, 'O-o-o, don't try to distract me with sex.' OK, so I wanted to sleep with you. Now I don't. Good night."

Barbara Dilman spent the night at the hospital, in a room down the hall from her stepdaughter. Her sister stayed with her, in the other twin bed. Around 3 A.M., the sister heard Barbara moan something in her sleep. It sounded like *not divorce*.

Alison Moffat shook two Amytals out of her bottle of sleeping pills, then decided she could do without them tonight.

Doug Brill, who had picked up Barbara's sister at the airport and driven her straight to the hospital, went back afterward to his borrowed house and got drunk on eleven-year-old brandy. At some point he chanted like a high school cheerleader:

"Shish kebab, shish kebab, biff, boom, bam!
Good old Larry's now roast lamb."

# 19

Lawrence Dilman's obituary in the Sunday *Times* was three columns wide and fulsome. It listed most of his books and all of his wives.

Of the books, *Wayward the World* got the biggest play: "published thirty-five years ago and hailed by critics as a notable advance in the genre of autobiographical first novel about a young man's sexual experience." Of the wives, Madeline Brill, "the well-known actress," was featured.

Lucy read it with her third cup of coffee and thought, If they'd listed his love affairs the way they did in that obit of Alma What's-her-name, Alison would have had star billing.

It was gratifying to know so much more about Larry than the know-it-all *Times*. The *Times* not only didn't know whom he'd slept with, it said he'd died of a heart attack. Lucy looked again at the accompanying photograph, of a twenty-years-younger Larry, and thought, His lips were always too thick. She remembered telling her husband once, "It would be like kissing a rubber suction cup."

The line pleased her all over again now, and she

was sorry she couldn't repeat it to Alison, or ask, in the interests of scientific research, "Was it like that?"

She tried to remember what Willard's mouth had looked like, but she couldn't even picture Willard's face clearly; Alison's husband had had a forgettable face. *But he was right for me. He was solid and kind and totally honest. But after he found out about Larry and me....*

Poor Alison, starved for admiration, latching onto Jeff Solent. I'm damned if I'll be the kind of Medicarean who grabs a bearded baby. Jeff must be forty years younger.

How old was Georgina Hampter, mid-fifties? If she was sentenced to—what, twenty years?—for manslaughter, then she wouldn't be eligible for parole till—. Lucy shivered and turned back to the first section of the *Times*, to make sure she hadn't missed any story on the murder. The inspector had still been keeping the lid on that news last night.

She wondered if he'd finally got some sleep. She had looked out her bedroom window at 7 A.M. to make sure his car was there, because she hadn't heard him come in. When she checked from the kitchen window soon after 8:30, the car was still there. Now it was 9:15, and much as she wanted him to knit his raveled sleeve of care, she felt he owed her a full report—damn soon.

But when he appeared on the terrace ten minutes later, the first thing he said was, "Joan's able to talk. I'm on my way to the hospital."

She got the feeling not just of a man in a hurry, but a man who is glad to have an excuse for being in a hurry so he won't have to talk. All the questions she'd had on the tip of her mind were dried up by his curtness. But then, as if sensing her frustration, he said,

"The letters were still there. Thanks to you, I found them. You were totally right about that."

She heard his emphasis of *that* and resented it enough so that she said, "I hope you had the sense to arrest Georgina last night."

"She's already out on bail."

"They set bail for a murder charge?" she asked incredulously.

"It wasn't a murder charge," he said, and bolted for his car.

"Was that the inspector?" To Lucy's astonishment, Alison was wearing a suit and carrying an overnight bag; she looked raddled, as if she'd slept in her makeup.

"Where are you going?"

"I'm moving to the Inn. Tell the inspector I thought it would be more convenient to stay there while I'm taping the scenes with Jeff. Jeff's picking me up at nine forty-five, so I'll just have coffee and juice."

From the depth of Lucy's hurt and indignation, the words shot out. "You can damn well get breakfast at the Inn. I'm tired of fixing meals for people on the run."

Alison sat down and said slowly, "I don't blame you. I haven't behaved nicely at all, this visit, but I can't help it."

"You're acting like a teen-ager with a crush. It doesn't make sense."

"It does. You have to believe that. I know what I'm doing."

"I've just been reading Larry's obituary," Lucy said, not too obliquely. She held out the *Times* folded to Larry's photograph. "Madeline Brill gets a mention: 'well-known actress,' et cetera."

Alison glanced at it and snorted. "Maddy will wear widow's weeds from Givenchy and throw herself on the grave to oblige the photographers." She dropped the paper on a table. "Did the inspector mention Georgina Hampter?"

"She's already out on bail! They didn't even book her on a murder charge. Can you imagine? I'll bet she goes through with that meeting tomorrow night."

"Good," Alison said absently. "Here's Jeff now."

He got out of the little green Karmann Ghia with the dented fender and stood there irresolutely, as if bracing himself, before he came over to the terrace. "Good morning, Mrs. Ramsdale."

His voice sounded so strained, so unlike his easy directness when he'd first met Lucy at the Dilmans', that she felt more compassion than anger.

"How's your pretty girl?"

"Not speaking to me." He was looking at Alison. "She thinks you faked an alibi for me. And I'd promised to take her into New York tomorrow to buy replacements for those books—but I had to tell her I'll be working with you on recordings."

"Would you like to back out?" Alison said, in a somber voice.

"No." The *no* was very quiet, but it gave a sense of commitment. "She'll get over this in a day or two. Anyway, she can't replace the books till after the meeting."

"Oh, yes, the meeting. Lucy, I'll talk to you there."

Lucy was so exasperated by this high-handed dismissal she was about to say, Don't bother, I may not even be there, when Alison came over to do the cheek-rubbing ritual women go through so they won't mess each other's makeup. What startled Lucy into silence was that Alison had tears in her eyes—her magnificent eyes. "Good-bye, darling; God bless. Thank you for everything. And don't feel cross that Madeline Brill rated a notice in Larry's obituary."

"You're a hell of a lot better actress," Lucy said. "You always were and you always will be."

Alison turned back to pat Lucy's cheek, and just for a second the old, mischievous glint shone out. "Even you don't know how good I am." Then, in a very slow voice, she said, "Look after your inspector. He'll need you."

As Lucy watched the tail of the little green car disappear in a blur, she said furiously, "God damn it, now *I'm* bawling."

Rather than submit to this weakness, she marched to the garage, got the clippers and a basket, and went forth to tackle the lilacs.

By the time she'd filled the basket almost full of purple lilacs and moved on to the newly luxuriant bush of whites McDougal had lavished manure on, she was feeling much better. She stood on tiptoe to reach a promising branch over her head and whacked it off. But instead of dropping it into the basket, she stared at it.

Why had Alison said dainty *white* blossoms? She'd said she and Jeff had been too busy talking to notice the oleander in the greenhouse. Then how had she known the flowers were white? Oleander was much more apt to be pink or reddish. Lucy thought, Even I wasn't sure what that bush was till I looked at the shape of the leaves. But there *are* some white oleanders. I'm sure there are. She must have seen them in California. It doesn't mean a thing. She just said whatever came into her head.

But then why did she lie about the bracelet charm? She didn't lose the clown; she lost the bird in the cage. If somebody found it near the oleander . . . Jeff. Jeff had got it back to her at lunch Saturday. Lucy remembered, with chilling clarity, how the inspector had examined the bird charm at dinner and made it sing *tweet*. Somehow he'd known Jeff had found it first—and where. Alison hadn't faked the alibi for Jeff; she'd faked it for herself. *We were together every minute*. But Alison couldn't possibly *murder* anybody. It was too fantastic even to think of.

# 20

Joan Dilman's head was still turbaned in bandages, but she was propped up in bed and her greeting to the inspector had a determined jauntiness. "Whoever designed these hospital gowns must have hated women, especially women with long necks. But I deserve it, after being so stupid last night. I tripped over a lamp cord in Larry's office and went down with a crash. In fact, I went out like a light."

She giggled nervously.

McDougal thought, She's been rehearsing that all morning. He said gently, "You were hit over the head. We know who did it. She's already been charged."

"I don't have to press charges, do I?"

"Why do you want Mrs. Hampter to go free?"

"Because Larry"—her veneer of calm cracked— "Larry was horrible to her. I heard him. I'd just started downstairs and they were in the back hall; it was before he took her into his office. He said, 'Some people burn old love letters, but I couldn't bear to get rid of yours. They're priceless. I want to read you a few choice gems before I give them to the—the AP man.'"

Joan wiped her eyes with the sleeve of her hospital gown.

McDougal handed her the small box of tissues from the bed table.

"I didn't want to listen. Truly I didn't. But I had to stay there."

He could see her frozen on the stair landing, trapped into hearing her father use blackmail.

"She was *begging* him. It was awful. And then Mrs. Terrizi came to get something out of the closet next to the phone alcove, and Larry took Mrs. Hampter into the office, and Mrs. Ramsdale was using the phone and I was so afraid she'd hear. I—I didn't want her to know my father was like that, Inspector. I didn't want anybody to know. He wasn't a nice man—and now I hate everything he wrote. I'm glad Mrs. Hampter burned *Wayward the World.*"

"You aren't really," McDougal said. "Some of our greatest writers were stinkers. There's no connection at all. Later, you'll be proud of his books all over again."

Her long nose was pink and polished from being wiped. She wadded the tissue into a ball. "I'd built him up so much in my mind, all those years I hardly ever saw him. I kept thinking how happy I'd be if I could just live with him all the time. And when he was sarcastic and mean and did things that hurt me—like he'd invite me to go someplace and then skip it if he got something better to do—I'd keep making excuses for him. I know that sounds incredibly stupid."

"Not to me. If you've loved somebody very much, you do go on making excuses. I've done it myself, for too long."

Joan's eyes widened. "You have? You aren't just saying that to make me feel better?"

"No. I never admitted it to anybody before. And now that I've told you, I'm the one who feels better. There's a time when we have to stop making excuses for somebody else. You found it out sooner than I did. And that's helped me make up my mind."

She smiled at him radiantly. "I'm glad. At first I was scared of you. Well, not exactly scared, but sort of awed. And I told you Barbara could have killed Larry because I wanted to make myself seem interesting. Anyway, I was jealous because Barbara was so broken up when Larry died; she doesn't show things but I knew. And I wanted to feel that way too—and I couldn't. But I didn't really mean what I said about the shish kebab. Did Mr. Brill tell you?"

"He delivered your message right away."

"Barbara's always tried to be nice to me. The thing is, you can always feel her trying. Do you know what I mean?"

McDougal kept a straight face. "Yes." He thought it was an inspired description.

"But she wasn't just trying to be nice to Larry, she was crazy about him. I used to see her look at him. She acts sort of brisk and bossy, and I was furious that she'd told him not to leave me money outright in his will because I'd do something foolish with it. I have a *right* to do something foolish if I want to."

The inspector had been manfully resisting the urge to smoke in a hospital room. Now he lit a cigarette and looked around for an ashtray.

"Use that glass on the tray," Joan said. "The nurse will bring me another. They want you to drink a lot of liquids but it gets very boring, just drinking and running to the bathroom and drinking. . . . I'm sorry if you're disappointed I won't press charges against Mrs.

Hampter, but I feel somebody in the family has to make up for what my father did to her. I hope she got her letters back."

"Eventually she will."

"I was going to burn them myself. That's why I insisted on going back last night to shut the windows. I went straight to Larry's office." She felt her bandaged head and said ruefully, "That woman needn't have hit me so hard."

"She didn't mean to hurt you. She panicked."

"Poor thing. I'll have a cigarette, please."

McDougal came near asking, Are you allowed to? but decided against it. He hoped the nurse wouldn't come in. He handed over his pack and reached to give her a light. Joan didn't inhale; she blew smoke in small huffs and puffs.

"Mrs. Hampter didn't kill Larry, you know. She couldn't have done all that stuff with the substitute skewer because she didn't have time. I was watching out an upstairs window—I mean, I wasn't watching *for* anything, I was just standing there staring—and I saw her go into the greenhouse, and then just a little while later I saw her go down the back path. I didn't see her actually come out of the greenhouse, but I saw her leave for home."

McDougal said, "By 'a little while later,' how much time do you figure it really was?"

Joan took a few more small huff-puffs while she considered. "Well, I went into the bathroom and washed my face in cold water and used Eye-gene so I wouldn't look so bleary. And I put on fresh makeup and powdered around my eyes. I knew Barbara would come up to look for me before dinner, and I didn't want her to know I'd been crying because she'd ask me why and I couldn't tell her. I didn't want to eat with the others, but that meant I'd have to—" She stopped dead, then went on carefully. "If I said five or six minutes, I'd only be guessing. I'm afraid I'm not a very good witness."

"You're a fine witness because you don't twist the truth around or say what you don't know to be a fact."

He must have expected her to look pleased because he was surprised and puzzled by her reaction: she literally cringed, as if he'd slapped her.

"I'm not all that honest," she muttered. "But if I only *guessed* who fixed up the skewer and don't tell you, that's not being an accessory, is it?"

"Of course not."

His cigarette was getting perilously short, but he didn't want to disturb their odd rapport by tamping it out in the glass. He lowered his hand and pinched surreptitiously with his fingers.

"I think I already know the murderer," he said, trying to sound matter-of-fact. "But if you saw anything at all"—he took a flying leap—"for instance, if you went down to the kitchen after Mrs. Hampter left to make yourself a sandwich so you could tell your stepmother you'd already eaten ..."

He knew from her involuntary jerk that he'd hit on something.

"You'd better tell me," he said quietly.

"Anybody could have been in the kitchen. It wouldn't have to mean that she—the person—was guilty. Anyway, I don't *believe* it. Because later, at dinner...."

Several minutes later she lay back against the pillows, looking tired but peaceful.

"I'm glad you'd already figured it out yourself. She was so sweet to me at dinner, and I didn't want to be the one to tell on her."

"It's our secret." He held out his hand. "Is that a deal?"

They shook hands solemnly.

"Are you going to put a cop outside my door? That's what they do in books."

"We'll put a cop somewhere else. In fact, I already have."

Jeff Solent had been peering into his rearview mirror. "I think I'm being tailed."

Alison said, "It doesn't matter. We'll have enough time to do what has to be done."

# 21

"Hi, Miss Coving. Is Mr. Solent here? I have to see him." The Evans child was still wearing blue jeans. So was Marcy Coving.

Marcy didn't say, Come in. She said, "No, he isn't," in a shutting-out voice.

"Do you know where he might be? It's very important. I have to show him something right away." Peggy Evans was clutching a printed sheet that looked like an advertising flyer. "One of the kids in our Riding Club got a copy for me, and I wanted Mr. Solent to see it so he could write an answer or something before the meeting. We *have* to do something because a lot of parents will blow their stacks when they see it and they'll back Mrs. Hampter and—look, let me show you."

In the small living room, the youngster drank a Coke in thirsty slurps while Marcy read the flyer. It didn't take long to read. The headline screamed in twenty-four-point type: DO YOU WANT YOUR CHILD POLLUTED WITH THIS?

"This" was a half dozen of the "dirty passages" Sergeant Terrizi had told Marcy about the day before, as relayed by Zora. Yanked out of context, from the confiscated books, they made rather startling reading.

"That woman!" Marcy said. "I could kill her."

"Mother says somebody should have knocked off Georgina Hampter instead of Lawrence Dilman. You and Mr. Solent were there that night, weren't you?"

"Yes." She watched her visitor fish out an ice cube to lick and shivered from another kind of cold. If somebody had expected Georgina to stay at the Dilmans' for dinner that night and had sharpened the substitute skewer even before she arrived. . . . "Did you try Jeff's apartment just now?"

Peggy Evans said delicately, "I thought I'd come here first, in case he was taking you to church or the beach or something."


Jeff opened the door of his apartment just long enough to come into the hallway and then closed it instantly behind him. Marcy hadn't seen him in almost twelve hours, and she was appalled at how haggard he looked.

Peggy Evans thrust out the flyer. "We thought you'd want to see this right away. Mrs. Hampter's going to have it handed out before the meeting."

"Is she?" he said, in a flat tone. "Sorry, I don't have time to look at it now."

"But the meeting's tomorrow night."

"Don't you think I know it?" He was suddenly almost shouting.

Peggy Evans backed away, still clutching the sheet of quotes.

"Jeff! Jeff, come back here." The voice carried through the closed door as clearly as it had once carried to a theater's top balcony. "How do you turn off this infernal machine? It's whiffling at me."

"Have fun with your recording session," Marcy said. "It's a pity we disturbed you for something so trivial." She turned and marched down the hall.

Inspector McDougal arrived a half hour later, but he stayed considerably longer.

Around two, he was with Chief of Police Salter at headquarters. The two men munched soggy sandwiches and drank coffee that tasted of soggy cardboard. "I've had three or four biddies come storming in here to say, 'How dare you arrest that great defender of decency, Georgina Hampter?' I'm tempted to say straight out why we nabbed her, but then I'd have had to spill the stuff about the love letters and you said to keep that quiet."

"Her gang wouldn't believe it anyway. She's already made herself out a martyr."

"You don't think we could lean on Joan Dilman to change her mind and press charges?"

McDougal shook his head. "Joan's already been through enough. And she has to feel she's making up for her father's blackmail."

Chief Salter tossed a cardboard container at the wastebasket beside his desk and missed. He leaned down heavily to retrieve it. "Be kind of awkward anyway, with all the support Georgina's got in this town. It isn't as if she's mixed up in the murder. Did you get all the dope you wanted from the police in Beverly Hills?"

"I had it before I went to Solent's apartment."

Sergeant Terrizi said to his bride-to-be, "And you can tell Mrs. Ramsdale I have to work straight through on the case with the inspector and you were lonely, so you thought you'd stop by and see her. Tomorrow's her shift at the Thrift Shop, so that's taken care of, but today you've got to make sure she doesn't run loose."

Angie was not only an enchantingly pretty girl, she took to emergencies as a bird takes to the air. And, once aloft, she was capable of sustaining quite a remarkable flight of improvisation. ". . . So I wanted you to look at these ads of bridal gowns," she said to Lucy, "because you have the best taste of anybody around here and I need your advice."

None of the wedding dresses in the ads suited Lucy's idea of what Angie should wear to the altar. In no time she had got out her drawing pad and was sketching a design that made Angie croon with pleasure.

For one thing, it wasn't just a design; it was Angie in the dress, and a very good likeness indeed.

"I know a little seamstress who'll make it for you," Lucy said. "Actually, she's biggish, but seamstresses are always supposed to be little—probably because they used to be paid starvation wages."

With the problem of a wedding dress settled, Angie moved to a new ploy. "Nicky's always telling me what a fabulous cook you are, and I wondered if you'd give me a few of your recipes."

But on this, she hit a dry hole. Lucy, the kind of cook who operates more on instinct and tasting than with measuring spoons, was bored with the whole idea. "If you'd like to come watch me sometime when I'm doing a special dish . . . right now I want to go over to the hospital and see Joan Dilman."

At 9 P.M. Angie reported to the inspector and Terrizi at headquarters. ". . . While she was getting a bunch of lilacs from the kitchen, I let the air out of her left rear tire. When she saw that tire, she let loose. Wow, can she lay it on! Then I said why didn't I drive her to the hospital in my car, and she calmed down some. The nurse said Joan Dilman wasn't allowed any visitors yet, so Mrs. Ramsdale left the flowers with a note. Then I had to drive her to the Inn because she wanted to see Miss Moffat, but the clerk said Miss Moffat wouldn't be in till late. So I drove her back home, and by then she seemed pretty down in the dumps. She asked me to come in for a drink; I offered to fix them and I made hers pretty strong. Then she said she didn't feel like eating alone—"

Lucy's figured it out, the inspector thought, but she still can't believe it. He wondered again if he was handling this the right way—if he shouldn't talk to her ahead. But he had given his word.

"—and so I warmed up the manicotti I'd brought her from Mama Terrizi and made a salad, and she had me open a bottle of wine, and she talked about old times in Greenwich Village till she got so yawny I couldn't think up an excuse to stay any longer. But she said she was going right to bed, and I waited down the road till I saw her upstairs light go out. Oh, and Nicky—you're to tell Marvin at the Exxon station to come put on her spare tire in the morning."

"Marvin will be too busy," Sergeant Terrizi said. "I'll arrange that."

# 22

The lights in the high school auditorium were so harsh Lucy's eyes stung. It was one more annoyance piled on a day of nagging worries. The garage man hadn't showed to put on the spare tire. She'd had to get a lift into town with Liz Carmody, who had probed for details of Larry Dilman's murder. "Come on, Lucy, don't be stingy. We know you always have the inside dope."

As Liz said later to other volunteers at the Thrift Shop, "Girls, I warn you, Lucy's in a foul temper. Don't ask her any questions about anything."

The volunteers circumvented this by an even more maddening (to Lucy) approach. The news that Lawrence Dilman hadn't died of a heart attack was too fresh and tempting a topic to abstain from, so they simply asked questions of each other, watching for Lucy's reaction: "Did you hear the police went to Jeffrey Solent's apartment? . . . Do you suppose he's the one? . . . Is it true Joan Dilman collapsed from nervous strain and is in the hospital? . . . Do you think it was really that, or did Joan find out something about the murder?"

For Lucy, who was used to being at the center, this was cruel and unusual punishment. But for once she didn't want to talk, or rather, the only people she wanted to talk to were unavailable. Alison hadn't returned her calls. McDougal had returned her call only secondhand; Sergeant Bayles had phoned and delivered the message: "If your car isn't fixed, a police driver will take you to the meeting and the inspector will join you there. Please save him a seat on the aisle."

The auditorium was so packed Lucy had to fight off a parade of latecomers who asked, "Is this seat taken?" and wouldn't take yes for an answer. Between fending them off, she glanced over the flyer somebody had thrust into her hand at the entrance; this had raised her blood pressure considerably, and so did the comments of people around her, discussing the excerpts quoted. It was the "Can you imagine this smut being handed out by a school librarian?" sort of thing.

They weren't people she knew; almost every face in the audience, or at least the ones she could see, was unfamiliar and, she thought, vulgar, common, ignorant. She knew she was being a snob, and unfair, but she felt like making a wide, dark distinction between them and herself—"our sort." She was baffled that McDougal had made such a point of her coming to the meeting. Her earlier indignation over the book burning and Georgina Hampter was submerged in far more personal anxieties and concerns. Alison had said, "I'll talk to you at the meeting," but how in God's name could they have any serious private talk in a place like this? And Lucy suspected the inspector was dodging the issue in the same way. She resented his avoiding her all day and then issuing that summons through Bayles, but waiting till the last minute to arrive.

He was inexcusably late; the nine members of the school board had filed in and were sitting on stage with the superintendent of schools. McDougal slid into the aisle seat just as Georgina came to the podium. She had a new, elaborate hairdo, and she dipped her head right, left, right, to acknowledge the applause. There were a few boos, but she ignored these and kept a set expression that might have been sprayed to hold, like her hair.

Lucy muttered out of the side of her mouth to McDougal, "Where the hell have you been?"

When she turned, she was startled to see his face —grim, grayish-white, so drawn he looked ten years older.

"Did you see Alison?"

He nodded, but he was looking straight ahead.

"What did she say? She promised to be here tonight."

People around them *sh-sh*-ed loudly; Georgina was already speaking. The inspector said, "Not now."

Lucy was too edgy to take in more than snatches of the opening speech, which was delivered in the tone of an evangelist warning of the dangers of Hell.

". . . just a few examples of the kind of filth, on this sheet you received at the door . . . depraved language . . . distorted, ugly picture of our own beloved United States of America . . ." And finally, in a coldly righteous tone, "The superintendent of schools has asked that the supporters of these books, who would foist them on our youth, be allowed to present their case."

At that point, Lucy thought she saw Jeff Solent standing in the wings right of stage. She had somehow assumed he'd be sitting with Alison, and now she scrutinized the backs of heads in the seven or eight

rows in front of her, then wriggled around to look behind and to both sides, trying again to locate her
friend. Once the inspector turned, as if he were about
to say something, but he didn't.

Georgina had sat down next to Superintendent
Bolling. The member of the school board Lucy had
campaigned for, Jenny Wright, got up and spoke briefly
on the need to let students exercise "the greatest priv-
ilege in a democracy—the right to think for themselves.
We cannot submit to censorship by whim."

She had barely finished when another member of
the school board, a man in a Hawaiian sports shirt,
jumped up and strode forward. "If my kid brought
home one of those books, he'd get his behind blistered.
Maybe Mrs. Hampter acted kind of out of line. But it's
our fault we didn't remove those books sooner, and I
back her one hundred percent. We've put up with this
permissive stuff too darn long, and I say, end it right
now."

Lucy, watching for another glimpse of Jeff Solent,
was momentarily deflected when Marcy Coving came
out from the opposite wing onto the stage. She was
holding several sheets of notes which she placed carefully on the podium. Her pale blond hair hung to her
shoulders, and she looked very young and tensely earnest. Something about the way she braced her shoulders made Lucy think of a prisoner in the dock: *Have
you anything to say before sentence is pronounced?*

"I want to give you just one or two examples of
how these passages have been pulled out of context to
give a false impression. For instance, the quote about
rape from *Soul on Ice* makes it sound as if Eldridge
Cleaver was bragging about his crimes. But a few para-
graphs later, he writes, 'After I returned to prison, I
took a long look at myself and, for the first time in my

life, admitted that I was wrong, that I had gone astray —astray not so much from the white man's law as from being human, civilized—' "

A woman in the third row jumped up and screamed, "Maybe *you* wouldn't mind a big black nigger grabbing you! You give our kids a few more books like this, and no decent woman will be safe."

Suddenly the place was a bedlam: cheers, boos, shouts. "Right on!" "That's telling 'em!" "Let the librarian finish." "This is a free country." "Dirty hippies—perverts—"

Georgina Hampter kept her seat and made no attempt to interfere. She looked rather pleased. Superintendent Bolling rose and held up his hand for silence but was answered by a fresh round of boos.

Marcy Coving stood her ground and tried to speak but was drowned out. Jeff motioned to her from the wings, and she went to him, walking with her head held high.

And then a new voice rose astonishingly, commandingly, above the din.

"Do you want to know who killed Lawrence Dilman? Listen!"

Lucy clutched the inspector's arm. "Alison! They'll mob her."

McDougal put his hand over Lucy's and held it there firmly. "Listen."

The hush was uncanny. It was as if the whole audience were holding its concerted breath.

"This is a tape-recorded confession which you are the first to hear. My name is Alison Moffat, and some of you have seen me in plays or movies. But this time, it's not make-believe. I killed Lawrence Dilman. I poisoned him. I only meant to make him sick for a day or two, but ignorance is no excuse, when you play with poison. So Lawrence Dilman is dead."

The hush broke. A buzz of voices took over until the magnificent voice said ringingly, "Murder! You're shocked! And you should be. For my own personal reasons, I wanted a man punished, and I appointed myself to do it. I took the law into my own hands, and I am a criminal. But when Georgina Hampter takes the law into *her* hands—burns a few books, chops off a few more of our individual rights—why aren't you just as shocked? You who agree with Georgina don't think of yourselves as killers, do you? You wave the flag and tell how you love this country. Most of you don't mean to wipe out our freedoms—any more than I meant to kill Lawrence Dilman. But we've had too much of men in government who take the law into their own hands. They've weakened our democracy. Don't help kill it. Because when you're left with the corpse—when you see what you've done—*it will be too late.*"

The last words were said so quietly, with so terrible a sense of despair, that the audience seemed stunned for two or three seconds after.

Then the noise rose like a tidal wave.

Lucy said to the inspector, "I have to go to her. Where is she?"

But even before McDougal spoke, Lucy read it in his face: Alison had given her final exit line.

# 23

"It was sleeping pills," Jeff said. "She was wearing that crazy costume she had on the night we met her—even the damn bracelet—and the odd thing is, she looked as if she were smiling." His voice broke. "She'd told the inspector she'd give herself up right after the meeting. But he must have begun to worry around the same time I did, and he went to check on her. . . . If I'd only realized ahead, I could have saved her."

"Saved her for what?" Marcy said gently. "For the stomach pump and the trial and the plain prison uniform? She'd have hated that."

Some of the strain went out of Jeff's face. "She even hated the idea of going to headquarters and "dictating a dreary confession like some stupid common criminal." We were having lunch at the Inn; that's when she told me what had happened. And in the lobby after lunch, she spotted one of those screamy-meemy placards announcing the meeting of Citizens for a Clean-Minded Community. She got the idea for the taped confession right then. God, she was marvelous. When we were working on the tape, she said to me once, 'If there's anything I hate, it's a bad third-act curtain.' She must have done thirty takes on that last line before she was satisfied. She said, 'It's got to be done so quietly it will explode like a time bomb.'"

"It did," Marcy said. "And she knew it would. So she didn't have to wait around afterward. She gave her greatest performance—and retired."

Jeff put his can of beer down hard on the table. "The thing is, if I'd gone right into the greenhouse with her, the way she wanted— But Mrs. Terrizi dumped another bag of briquets on the fire and damn near put it out. So big chief know-how Solent had to do his fire dance and get the thing going again." He grimaced. "When I finally got to the greenhouse, I couldn't figure out where Alison had gone. I saw the gold charm—the bird—on the floor and stuck it in my pocket. Then Alison came in the other door and said she'd gone to the kitchen to see what time it was. She started spilling out how I mustn't be upset by Dilman; he'd always been a chaser. She said, 'Once he even chased me— and caught me.' I was standing there with my eyes bugging out while she told me how Dilman smashed up her marriage. So I forgot all about the charm till the next day, in your apartment. And then, when the inspector said Miss Moffat had given me an alibi for the time in the greenhouse, I palmed the bloody thing to keep him from seeing it. I had to get it to Alison right away. That's why I ran out on you."

Marcy made soothing noises, the of-course-dear-I-understand-perfectly sort.

"And at lunch Alison told me what had happened. She said I was the only one she could trust. What a woman!" He shook his head. "Can you imagine her ever falling for a show-off bastard like Dilman?"

233

After the smallest hesitation, Marcy said, "Incredible."

The Associated Press stringer had got a scoop beyond his wildest dreams. All the morning papers carried his story. Even the *Today* show gave him a nod. Douglas Brill read the AP account in the *Times* and said to Lucy later that morning, "Alison's getting the biggest reviews of her life. What a way to go!"

The school board issued a dignified statement for the next issue of the *Wingate Bugle*: "In view of the unfortunate publicity stemming from the meeting on controversial books, the Board of Education has decided to postpone its next vote on the volumes in question till the fall term."

The Association of Concerned Citizens for a Clean-Minded Community issued a statement too, or a proclamation, through its chairperson, Georgina Hampter: "Parents! Will you listen to the rantings of a confessed murderer and stop fighting against filth? Or will you rise up and exercise your rights as free citizens? It is up to YOU to decide what kind of books your sons and daughters will read. Eternal Vigilance was the motto of our Founding Fathers. Be Vigilant! Act!"

Lucy flung the *Bugle* down on the terrace. "A week ago I was reading bits aloud to Alison and it all seemed so ludicrous. And when she told me she'd had an affair with Larry—I never told you that, did I?"

"She told me herself," the inspector said. "She talked very freely. It was a relief to her to spill it all out. She'd wanted to tell you the truth as soon as she heard Dilman was dead, but she didn't think it was fair to involve you."

He could hear Alison saying, "And I couldn't let Lucy know she was the one who put the idea into my head in the first place. I'd been furious, seeing Larry up to his old tricks, and Lucy said, 'Oh, as soon as he gets a bellyache he'll go running back to Barbara.' I was waiting for Jeff in the greenhouse, and the minute I saw that oleander. . . . A neighbor of mine in Beverly Hills had been sick as a dog after some idiot did a shish kebab with oleander. But you know that; you checked with the police out there. It was nice of you to realize I hadn't meant to kill Larry."

Maybe not consciously, the inspector had thought. So you conveniently "didn't know" what oleander would do to a heart condition.

"If only I hadn't made her go to Larry's for dinner," Lucy said now.

"Nobody *makes* anybody do anything. She wanted to go. She told Solent she'd wanted to see Dilman 'caught in old age like a rat in a trap.'"

Lucy was staring unseeingly at the white lilac bush. Finally she said, "Alison was part of the happiest period of my life, and nothing will ever be the same again. I feel as if I'm finished too."

It was so unlike Lucy, who savored the present like a greedy child and begged for second helpings, that McDougal knew drastic measures were called for.

"I have no right to inflict my troubles on you," he said, "especially when you're already feeling depressed. But you're the only person I can talk to— about what happened when I went in to meet Eileen."

"Of *course* you must talk." Lucy's voice had recovered some of the young, warm vitality he hadn't

235

heard in days. "I've been the selfish one, so wrapped up in my own feelings I acted as if I didn't give a damn about anything else. But I do, Mac—you know that."

She sat waiting expectantly.

McDougal hadn't known it would be so hard; he had to force the words out. "When I went into the Plaza to register, there was a message at the desk from Eileen, saying she was waiting in the Palm Bar and would I join her as soon as I'd checked in. I—well, I thought she'd taken an earlier plane because she'd been so impatient to see me. So I didn't even go up to the room. I left my bag and went straight to the bar." He closed his eyes for a second, as if it hurt to look at the sun. "Eileen was there, all right. She looked marvelous—ten years younger than when I'd last seen her."

Had a face-lift in Paris, Lucy thought, with a pang.

"She told me her husband had flown over with her." McDougal's voice was flat. "She'd changed her mind about coming back to me. But she wanted the three of us to have dinner together and be friends. When I refused, she said, Why couldn't I see reason?"

"Whenever they say that," Lucy said, "it always means they want you to see *their* reason. I don't think she was deliberately trying to be bitchy—not that she'd have to try. But she just wanted you to go on loving her no matter what she did. I hope you told her what a stinking trick she'd pulled."

"I didn't wait around to tell her anything." The words were coming more naturally now. "I went out to the desk to get my bag and take off. But the bag had already been sent up to my room. And a bottle of Scotch I'd bought. So I holed in there and got drunk.

But Terrizi phoned me about something—and later I decided to come home."

He said *home*, Lucy thought, and felt a radiant contentment.

"Eileen has called me here since," McDougal said. "She's changed her mind again. She's through with her husband; he's already gone back to Europe."

Lucy sat very still.

"I told her I was through too."

Lucy was still unnaturally quiet. She had half turned away from him.

He watched her in profile and improvised recklessly. "She asked me if there was another woman. And I said yes. Eileen said, 'Is she beautiful?'"

Lucy turned to look at him, and her eyes crinkled with laughter. "I hope you knew what to say to that."